DEAD AGAIN

A NORFOLK COZY MYSTERY

KEITH FINNEY

Keith Finney - Author

Dead Again

AN INVITATION

Welcome to your invitation to join my Readers' Club.

Receive free, exclusive content only available to members—including short stories, character interviews and much more.

To join, click on the link towards the end of this book and you're in!

BEGGAR MAN'S CAVE

"Can you think of anything better to do on a warm Saturday morning than be out and about in a vintage Morgan sports car?" Ant had to shout his question at Lyn to overcome the low rumble of the car's powerful engine.

"As a matter of fact... oh, what's the point?" She watched Ant mouth "eh?" before leaning into him. "Either stop and put the hood up or slow down so we can hear each other. Honestly, Anthony Stanton, sometimes I could—" Ant got the message and slowed the Morgan to a more sedate pace. "There, isn't that better, silly man. We're on a country lane in the middle of nowhere, not the Le Mans racetrack. While we're at it, tell me again why you've dragged me out so early on the first day of my summer holidays?"

Ant lifted his chin and frowned at his passenger.

Since I'm already in trouble, may as well go for it.

"I thought you said head teachers didn't take holidays, they just worked at a slower pace?" He had judged Lyn's reaction to a tee and only his quick thinking staved off one of her famed ear flicks, which he dreaded. "Anyway, we're not in the middle of nowhere."

Her eyes flared. "Don't change the subject. You may be a Lord, but it doesn't cut any ice with me." Lyn rearranged herself in her rich leather car seat and looked straight ahead. "Anyway, where are we, and more's the point, where are you taking me?"

Ant looked across and smiled, then looked to his front as Lyn glared at him for not watching the road. "Just around this bend and... yes, I think you'll recognise where we are."

The Morgan continued at its sedate pace as an ornate set of wrought-iron gates came into view, as did two armed police officers. Lyn's eyes were glued to an ornate hand-painted sign to the right of the gate:

Sandringham House - No Entry to the Public

She looked at Ant, then the police officers. "You have the wrong entrance and are going to get us shot, stupid man."

Ant revved the Morgan as an act of defiance and obeyed an assertive hand gesture from the female officer to come to a halt. Clutching the menacing matt-black submachine gun into her body, the officer leant into the Morgan. "Good morning, Lord Stanton. You are expected. May I just ask for a form of identification for the lady?"

Ant turned to Lyn and took in the unglamorous site of her jaw hanging half open."

"You have remembered to bring your passport, Lyn?"

The question shook Lyn out of her stupor. A look of panic now replacing her open mouth. "I... er, well..."

"Not to worry. I picked it up when I called around for you." Ant retrieved the document from his inside pocket.

As the female police officer compared Lyn's likeness with her passport, the second police officer busied himself circling the Morgan. Ant was unsure if it was part of a security check, or that the officer simply liked vintage auto-mobiles.

"That all seems to be in order, sir. Please park in the stable yard behind the house. You will be met as previously agreed. May I take any mobile phones that you have?" Ant gestured to his completely bemused companion, who complied without saying a word. "Thank you, sir." The officer stood back from the car, pointed in the direction of the ornate gates that were beginning to open, then saluted.

Ant returned the salute and gently urged the Morgan forward, reaching the entrance just as the still-moving gates allowed just enough space for his car to squeeze through.

"Are you going to tell me what all this is about, or am I here just for the ride?" Lyn's words demanded an answer.

Ant ignored the question for several seconds as the Morgan continued at a stately pace in keeping with the incredible surrounding of parkland, sweeping vistas of flower gardens, and in the distance, the majestic sight of Sandringham House, the Queen's Christmas residence.

"You've been here before. Why are you so surprised?" Ant gently swerved to avoid a pair of turtle doves who were far too preoccupied with each other to notice danger to life and limb.

"Yes, I have, but through the tourist entrance holding a guidebook and ice cream, not being waved through by armed police who were clearly expecting us, or should I say you?"

Ant smiled as he brought the Morgan back onto the narrow tarmac road which carved its way through the park like a ribbon of black silk through a sea of green. "They knew you were coming too. Why do you think I nicked your passport?"

One, two, three...

Lyn exploded. "And that's another thing, how dare you—"

"Oh, look at that. Isn't it magnificent?"

Lyn stopped shouting and followed Ant's extended finger. As they passed St Mary Magdalene Church to their right, the road swept down and to the left. A small lake revealed itself. The water's edge was broken by a thick carpet of brightly coloured vegetation and carefully placed rocks, which added to the rustic feel of the place.

"Isn't that fantastic, Lyn?" Ant didn't wait for an answer. He knew they were seconds away from rounding one side of Sandringham House and turning into the spacious stable yard, now used as a refreshment area and entrance to the museum. "This place will be full in a few hours, just as well we were told to be here early."

Lyn gave Ant a look of incredulity. "We? I think you mean The Lord Stanton."

Ant closed his eyes for a second just like a child who believed if they couldn't see their parents, their parents couldn't see them.

"Er, well, yes, I suppose you're right. But they'll look after you while I'm meeting, er..."

She immediately picked up on his faltering sentence. "Meeting whom, exactly? I assume it's someone rather important given where we are. Are you seeing a member of the—"

"You've guessed, Lyn. I should have known. Yes, you are right, I'm seeing a member of the Intelligence Corp. Haven't a clue what they want, but I told you months ago that the military never really let you go."

Lyn shot her friend a sceptical look. "Intelligence Corp my foot. You could have met them anywhere. You must think I'm stupid."

Before Ant had a chance to respond, he had brought the Morgan to a stop by a heavy half-glazed oak door, its frosted glass etched with the cipher of the Prince of Wales. Within seconds an immaculately turned-out footman in a dark blue tunic with red piping in his collar and cuffs appeared on Lyn's side of the car. "Good morning, sir, madam. Please allow me to show you through. Perhaps Ms Blackthorn would like to look around the museum, which you will have all to yourself?"

Ant climbed out of the car as the footman opened the door for Lyn.

"Sounds like a plan. Are you okay with that, Lyn? It should only take twenty minutes or so".

Get me in before she throws something at me.

Looking slightly perplexed at the footman using her name and offering unfettered access to thousands of arte-facts belonging to the Royal Family, she remained rooted to the spot as Ant disappeared into the Victorian building.

"So THAT'S IT, then. You're not going to tell me who you met?" Lyn's face thundered as they neared Sidbourne Deep, a long cliff-lined beach thirty minutes from Sandringham.

Ant smiled at Lyn enigmatically, knowing this would do little to placate his friend. "As I've said half a dozen times. There are some things I can't share even with you. I'm not being awkward or evasive. I took an oath and that's all there is to it."

Before Lyn was able to pursue the matter further, Ant brought the Morgan to a halt in a small public car park which had, at one end, an old wooden five-bar gate giving access to the beach.

"Come on, you said you wanted to fill your lungs with good Norfolk sea air. Well, now's your chance. Come on. Last one through the gate buys lunch." Ant had started to run before he'd finished making the challenge.

"That's not fair. You have a head start."

Ant looked back and waved as he sped towards the gate. He soon realised his mistake as he tripped over a protruding stone and fell head over heels onto the rough ground.

"Serves you right. Have you not read about the hare and the tortoise?" Lyn made the most of her good fortune and reached the gate as Ant continued to dust himself down from his fall. "And I want the full works for lunch, so I hope you've brought your wallet with you? See you on the beach."

By the time Ant had stopped rubbing his knee, having first looked around to make sure no one other than Lyn had seen him fall, he had lost sight of her. Limping, he passed through the gate and looked down a steep slope of loose sand.

That's all I need.

Two minutes and three stumbles later, Ant found himself on a firmer surface as he limped down to the shoreline across damp sand in an effort to locate Lyn. She was nowhere to be seen. As he looked around, he held a hand to his hair, for which the onshore wind had other ideas. Ant's gaze was drawn to the horizon as he watched two container ships and a bulk carrier glide slowly across his field of vision like ducks in a fairground shooting gallery.

"You took your time." Lyn's voice startled him as he turned to see his friend just yards way.

"Er, I've been here for several minutes while you've been hiding." Ant waved a hand around to emphasise his point.

"If you think I was going to hang around while you felt sorry for yourself, you can think again. Anyway, the cliffs are really interesting, you know, the way the sediment layers were laid down. Look, you can see about eight different layers. Fascinating, isn't it?" Lyn pointed to a long line of cliffs with alternating red, grey, and white stripes running through them.

Ant was far from impressed. "If you say so. Now, you were the one who wanted to stroll on the beach, so what's it to be, a lecture on sedimentary rocks or getting our feet wet?"

Lyn shook her head. "You are a philistine. Come on, Hopalong, let's get going"

Ant tried his hurt schoolboy look but quickly realised Lyn wasn't biting. The tactic, having backfired, made his sore knee worse as he hurried to catch up with his unsympathetic friend.

"Strange place name, Sidbourne Deep, don't you think?"

Ant struggled to hear what Lyn was saying in the stiffening north wind as he rubbed his right knee with one hand, all the time trying to keep up with his companion's brisk pace. "Normal for Norfolk, you mean. Just think of Wymondham and Tasburgh. They sound nothing like the way they're spelled. Dad reckons they did it on purpose during the Middle Ages to identify strangers. If you couldn't pronounce a place name like the locals, you must be an enemy."

Lyn smiled. "Always been an awkward lot, haven't we?"

"If you mean Boudica falling out with the Romans and Robert Kett's run-in with the king, I suppose you have a point, not that it ended well for either of them, did it?"

She smiled as Ant finally stopped limping and linked arms with her. "No, but I suppose there's a sort of nobility in standing up for yourself."

Ant laughed. "If you mean ending up in the mud of a

Roman battlefield or hanging from Norwich Castle, then yes, I suppose there is, except everyone else went home for tea while poor old Robert swung like a pendulum, and Boudica never saw Norfolk again after ransacking London."

"Well, well, I'd forgotten you were such a swot at history; about the only thing you did take an interest in at school if my memory serves me right."

Without warning, the heavens opened, catching them off guard. "What the... Come on, Lyn, let's make for Beggar Man's cave." He pointed at a small opening in the cliff face around fifty feet distant.

He could see Lyn straining to see where he was pointing to, such was the intensity of the squall. "Just beyond that upturned boat. Come on, let's get out of this weather before we catch our death."

Ant unlinked arms with Lyn and pulled her by the hand towards the cave entrance. As they neared the old boat, the sand gave way to a broad line of shingle. Ant swerved to one side and made a final push for the relative safety of the cave. "Thank heavens we're out of that. Here, take this to dry yourself." Ant passed Lyn a handkerchief.

She inspected the bedraggled fabric before accepting his gift. "And just how long have you had this in your pocket?"

Ant wore his hurt look. "Not that long, a couple of months... or so. Six at the most."

She shook her head, causing water droplets to spray over Ant.

"Steady on, girl. Anyway, beggars can't be choosers."

Lyn wrung out the square of cloth having rubbed her hair, then ran her hands through what had been, until a few minutes previously, shoulder-length flowing locks, now reduced to a series of stringlike braids.

"Then why is this called Beggar Man's cave?" Lyn's challenge made Ant laugh.

"That's clever… for you, anyway. Come here, give me that handkerchief." Without waiting, he grabbed the wizened fabric and started to rub it in a circular motion through Lyn's hair.

"Er, thank you, but no thank you. Left to you, I'll end up bald." Lyn pulled away from her helper and walked farther into the cave, what light there was fading as she walked deeper into the cliff.

Ant followed, straining to make out the uneven surface of the ancient excavation. "Suit yourself but don't moan to me when you come down with a cold."

Lyn let out a throaty laugh. "So says the king of man flu."

As their eyes became accustomed to the murky light, Ant felt compelled to run a hand over the jagged stone of the cave wall. "Notice anything?"

Lyn looked around, put a finger to her chin, and adopted a studious look. "Er, it's dark, or is that a trick question, Sherlock?"

"Not at all. No, I mean… look… this place is as dry as a bone. No seepage of water from the surrounding rock. I can see why old One-Arm Jake set up house in here."

Lyn once more scanned the space, her eyes flitting as minerals within the ancient rocks caught what light there was and sparkled. "Not a bad place for a beggar, I suppose. He must have done all right to have dossed here for so long."

"Guess you're right. Dad said he'd been told Jake lost his arm in WWI and when he came home the man couldn't cope with normal life after what he had experienced in France, so he lived out the rest of his life in here. I guess the locals must have brought him food and slipped him the odd penny. Sad, really."

The cave fell silent as Ant's words bounced around the hard surfaces before being lost in the dark.

"Come on, don't go into a decline on me. Let's see if it's stopped raining."

Lyn's words struck home and shook Ant out of his darker thoughts.

Straight to the truth of it as usual.

He followed Lyn to the cave mouth and scanned the horizon. The sky still looked threatening, promising more heavy downpours. "I always wanted to go to sea, you know. Pity I can't stand being seasick. Mind you, it didn't put Nelson off, did it?" Still taking in the majesty of the North Sea, he waited for Lyn to respond, half expecting her to rib him about throwing up when sailing on anything other than the calm of the Norfolk Broads. "Lyn, did you hear what I said?"

Still his friend didn't answer. Ant turned his attention from the incredible vista before him to see what Lyn was up to. "Lyn, you're as white as a sheet. What's wrong?"

"What? Yes... I, er, what were you saying?"

"For goodness' sake, woman, what's up with you?" He watched as she slowly began to move forward ignoring the lingering drizzle. She stopped about four feet away from the upturned boat that straddled the entrance of the cave. "Look."

Ant strained to see to what she was referring. "Look at what. Are you ill? This isn't like you."

Lyn didn't answer. Instead, she lowered herself to her knees. "It's hair."

By now Ant stood at her side and now understood what she meant. Silence once again fell as both friends tried to make sense of what they were looking at.

"It's rope, Lyn. I'm sure of it."

Lyn reached forward to touch the damp strands snaking out from underneath the broken vessel. "No, it's not, Ant. Someone is inside the boat."

Ant gently touched Lyn's hand to encourage the woman to let go of whatever it was.

Oh no. I think she's right.

"Lyn... Lyn, let go. There's only one way to find out, isn't there?" Ant put a hand under Lyn's elbow and helped her to her feet. "Come on, stand back, and I'll flip it over."

Doing as she was asked, Lyn stepped away from the sad scene and watched as Ant took hold of one edge, being careful to avoid the material Lyn had run through her fingers.

"Shouldn't we ring the police first?"

Ant turned to his friend, almost causing him to lose his grip of the boat. "And what if it is old rope, Lyn. Imagine what dear Inspector Riley would have to say." Not waiting for a response, Ant turned his attention back to righting the weather-beaten vessel. Loose paint flaked off as he manhandled the boat, leaving a scattering of red and white flakes on the shingle beneath. With one last heave, Ant flipped the vessel over and watched it rock back and forth until it found its balance. As he turned to look at what lay inside, he hoped against hope that he was right about the rope. He soon had his answer.

"What a terrible way to leave this world." Lyn moved forward as she spoke, her eyes fixed on the tragic scene.

2

TRINKETS AND MEMORIES

As the two sullen friends focused on the fully clothed body of a woman lying face down in the multi-coloured shingle, it was Ant who spoke first. "Now I think it's time to call the police. Do you want to do it or should I?" He turned to look at Lyn who was frowning.

"There's something about her that unsettles me, Ant, but I don't know why. Help me to turn her over." Lyn began to move forward.

Ant grabbed her arm. "Steady on, Lyn. You know better than that."

His sharp words and restraining hand brought her to an immediate stop. "Sorry, Ant. Don't know what got into me, it's just—"

He leant into her. Lyn responded by reciprocating. "I guess I'll make the call since you obviously didn't hear me." Ant bumped shoulders and offered a gentle smile. Lyn gave him a confused look then returned her attention to the woman.

"Yes, police, please." Ant gave the emergency call handler details of what they had found and their location.

"As soon as you can, please. In a few minutes this place will be full of the rubberneck brigade."

For now, they remained on their own getting soaked in the continuing drizzle. Ant looked out to sea. "I suppose the boat washed ashore in last night's storm. Looking at the water now it's hard to take in what that stuff is capable of. The question is why was a woman or anyone, for that matter, out on their own in a small boat on a night like last night?'

Lyn spoke quietly as if in a church. "You're supposing she was on her own? What if—"

"I didn't think of that, Lyn. Heaven forbid that was the case. One death is enough without thinking someone might be... well, anywhere out there."

Quiet fell over the friends again, both lost in their thoughts. The interlude didn't last long as Ant's prediction of a viewing gallery began to take shape. His attention was drawn to a man and woman fast approaching.

"Are you okay?" A second later the grey-haired man caught sight of the body and urged his wife to look away, which she ignored.

"Poor thing. Can't we cover her up to give the lady a bit of dignity?"

Ant shook he head. "The police are on their way and won't thank us for interfering with the crime scene."

The elderly lady unlocked arms with her husband and took a step forward. She spoke to Ant but kept her eyes on the woman lying before them in the sand. "Police? But the poor thing drowned. It's not a crime scene."

Her husband joined the woman. "I think what he means is that until the police have completed their initial findings, we should assume nothing, dear."

Ant nodded as the spritely lady turned on her husband. "Will you stop mansplaining. I'm not stupid, you know."

The elderly man shrugged his shoulders and looked to Ant for help.

"Let's make sure people are kept back, shall we. Anyone walking past will be naturally curious to find out what we are all looking at. It's important this area is left as undisturbed as possible until the police arrive, so that means us moving too." His intervention worked in distracting the man's wife from pursuing her grievance with her husband.

Stepping away from the sad scene, each scanned the beach for signs of strangers. For now, things remained quiet. Looking up at the cliff, the elderly man adjusted his peaked cap to keep the continuing drizzle from his eyes. "They say this place is cursed you know. Looking at that poor lady, Sidbourne Deep is certainly living up to its name."

The man's words sparked Ant's interest. "What's in a name? You surely can't believe in all that stuff?"

Adjusting his cap to provide better cover from the inclement weather, the old man gave Ant a wry smile. "You know, we are only a stone's throw away from Weybourne, which in Old English means felon's stream. It's said that criminals were made to kneel with their hands tied behind their backs and pushed into... well, you get the picture. Anyway, who's to say the stream just inland from here wasn't used for the same purpose. If folklore is to be believed, it was. Locals down the centuries believed this place is tainted and can bring bad luck, or worse, if you don't respect it."

Ant shook his head. "I hardly think this woman could be said to have disrespected anything, in fact, just the opposite. He turned to view the still frame of her body.

Before anyone had a chance to continue a conversation, the sound of police sirens pierced the damp air.

Two minutes later, Detective Inspector Riley arrived, walked straight past the four adults and came to a halt within a few feet of the corpse. Ant noticed several people on the beach, attracted by the police presence. On the clifftop stood someone with binoculars trained on the scene.

At least they have the decency to keep their distance.

As he was about to turn his attention back to the detective, he was amazed to see a woman waving a stick, running towards the man with binoculars. He stifled a chuckle as he watched her prey turn and run for it.

I'd love to know what she's shouting.

Riley turned to face the small gathering, concentrating on Ant and Lyn. "It's Saturday. We have a body, and what do you know, Punch and Judy have shown up; all's normal, then."

Ant resisted the urge to bite back.

"Well done," whispered Lyn before turning her attention to Riley. "Don't you think you should tone down the sarcasm? It was pure luck, if that's the right word, that we came across this before someone else did. So why don't we all take a deep breath and start again?"

"Well done, you too," whispered Ant.

Riley looked suitably chastened as Lyn's words hit home. He glanced at the other couple and gave an embarrassed smile, which Ant thought made the lady and gentleman even more uncomfortable as they moved closer to each other for mutual support.

The detective turned to Ant and Lyn. "Well, I suppose that might be a good idea... as long as you stay out of my way."

The pair failed to react.

"Good," added Riley. "Then we understand each other.

Now tell me how you found her." He looked at the body as he spoke.

Ant recounted what had happened. Riley exploded.

"You mean to tell me you interfered with police evidence by upending this boat?" His face turned purple with rage.

After giving Riley an exaggerated blink, which lasted a full three seconds, Ant responded. "And would you have been pleased if you had been called out to the mysterious case of the rope popping out of an upside-down boat three-quarters the way up a beach?"

Lyn and the other couple's shoulders rose in unison as they tried to stop themselves laughing. Riley looked from one to the other. "This woman is dead and all you lot can do is snigger?"

A solemn silence fell as his words sank in, that was except for Ant. "So, you admit the only way to find out if what we saw was old rope, or..."

The detective gave Ant a look of pure contempt. "That may be the case, but... listen, it's not for me to justify myself to you. A woman has drowned in a storm. My job is to identify her and inform her relatives of the tragedy. She was someone's daughter or, who knows, wife. You can tittle-tattle all you like. I've got a grown-up job to get on with, unlike some who seem to have too much time on their hands."

This time Ant wasn't prepared to hold back. "You assume too much, Detective Inspector Riley. Please do not measure the worth of others by your own standing. You may be disappointed with the result."

"So speaks the Lord of the Manor. What do you know of real life?"

"So speaks a policeman who usually can't tell the difference between an accident and a murder."

The two men began to square up to one another, nostrils flaring, and chests puffed out.

"Stop it, both of you. You're like a pair of peacocks arguing over who has the best plumage. Can I remind you there is a dead woman lying not six feet behind you, so grow up before I knock your heads together."

Lyn's intervention de-escalated matters within seconds. The two men, shoulders slumped, both looked at their shoes as if waiting to be called into the head teacher's office, which was precisely what she had intended.

Unseen by all present as tempers rose, was the arrival of the local press. Riley looked up to see a tall, slim woman writing at a furious pace on a notepad. Beside her a man had a camera up to his eye taking picture after picture. "If you print so much as a syllable of what you've heard or publish a single photograph, you will be for the high jump. Do I make myself clear?"

The photographer immediately put his camera down. The reporter was more stubborn. "Jemma Cole, lead crime reporter for the *North Coast Herald,* and this is Les Frost, accredited press photographer. We have a perfect right to be here, Officer."

Riley's eyes widened. "You have no right to be this close to a crime scene at this time, as well you know, so back off, and remember what I said about publishing one iota of what you have seen and heard here today. Norfolk Constabulary press office will issue a press release when I have concluded my initial findings, so you will have to wait until then, clear? And I am not an officer, I am a Detective Inspector. "

The reporter stopped scribbling and put the notebook in a large side pocket of her *Northface* jacket.

As Riley returned his attention to the body, Ant noticed

the reporter trying to catch his eye. Once he made contact, she nodded her head to one side in a conspiratorial manner. Unable to resist the intrigue of her movement, Ant began to move towards the confident woman. He caught sight of Lyn's look of disapproval.

"What?" he said quietly.

"I'll give you what. Just be careful. Remember who she is. Do you really want to be splashed all over the papers?"

She has a point, as usual.

Nevertheless, curiosity, and the prospect of spending a little time with an attractive young woman, tipped the balance in favour of taking the risk. Noting Riley now had his back to him, Ant quietly made off, causing the reporter to move several feet farther away from events and conceal herself behind a row of curious onlookers, and Riley's line of sight.

Holding her right hand out, the reporter reintroduced herself. Normally, Ant would have found this irritating given she had just announced herself in front of everyone. On this occasion he was prepared to overlook the matter.

"You can call me Ant, or Anthony if you want to be more formal."

"If I wanted to be formal, I would be addressing you as Lord Stanton, wouldn't I?"

Ant smiled. "I see you have done your homework."

Jemma returned Ant's smile allowing it to linger just long enough for him to notice. "That's my job. Oh, and I have a photographic memory, and I remembered reading an article on you about opening a training centre at Stanton Hall. I have to say, you are much better looking in person."

Ant could feel his cheeks flushing.

She doesn't mess about.

"Then you will understand why I ask people to call me

Ant. I can't be doing with all that title stuff; it places expectations in some people's mindset that I can't possibly live up to."

The reporter laughed. "Are you telling me you would prefer to give up your title. May I quote you?"

Ant began to inwardly panic as Jemma retrieved her notepad and licked the end of her pencil. "You most certainly cannot." His stern features bore into the reporter.

"Only kidding, er... Ant. But what about an interview?"

Ant looked back at Lyn, who was watching him with interest. He shrugged his shoulders to indicate disinterest with the reporter.

Lyn doesn't believe me.

"Why do you want to interview me? I'm just a farmer." He grinned like a little boy who had just been given a bag of sweets.

Jemma wagged a finger at him. "Hardly just a farmer. Let's see; a man due to inherit a large Norfolk estate and Grade I listed medieval Hall, local benefactor, interests in the city, and, oh, I nearly forgot, an ex-intelligence officer."

"You make me sound like a cartoon character."

She laughed again. "As I said, it's my job to dig out information."

"You mean dig the dirt."

"I mean exactly what I said. I think you have a story to tell that my readers will be interested in. Now, what do you say?"

Ant pondered matters for a few moments. He looked deep into her eyes as if attempting to discover her very essence. "Tell you what, I'll do you a deal."

Jemma's smile broadened. "I like deals, so what have you to offer?"

That woman is flirting with me.

"I'll give you an exclusive if you agree to do what the Detective Inspector told you to do. Now, do we have a deal?" Ant held his hand out to seal their understanding.

Jemma first looked at Ant, then his hand, before returning his eye contact. "Deal."

Just then, Ant heard Riley shouting loudly. Lyn was bent down by the body holding something. He made his way quickly back to Lyn as Riley continued his tirade.

"Don't you dare tamper with police evidence. Give me that or I will arrest you here and now. There may be fingerprints or DNA on that, which you have now compromised.

To Ant's surprise, Lyn didn't react. It was as if she hadn't heard Riley, or she didn't care.

"Lyn," he said quietly.

She looked up at him. Her eyes were beginning to fill with tears. She held out a silver bracelet with several lucky charms hanging from it. "It belongs to Amber Burton. I told you there was something about her I thought familiar even with her face buried in the sand."

"Amber Burton?" shouted Riley, his blood still up from his words with Lyn.

Lyn stroked the dead woman's hair. "As teenagers we were inseparable. I bought her this for her eighteenth birthday." She held the bracelet up to Ant. Riley intercepted it.

"Well, at least we have a name for her. Are you sure, before I send my officers on a wild-goose chase and frighten a set of parents out of their lives by giving them inaccurate information?" Riley's voice was quieter, more controlled now.

Lyn nodded. "But you don't understand, Amber Burton died ten years ago."

3

AN ANGRY FATHER

A lazy drizzle continued to hang in the air soaking everything it touched as Saturday morning turned into afternoon. Stanton Parva churchyard stoically resisted the inclement weather as it had done for a thousand years. All remained quiet, undisturbed by time as it continued to protect its precious guests.

"I know exactly where Amber's grave is." Lyn led the way, her casual canvas shoes soaked as she walked purposefully through the wet grass.

Ant recognised the signs of his friend's distress, a quiet resolve to get things done, a reluctance to give way to her emotions.

Never wants to show any weakness.

"Slow down, will you. I'm getting soaked." His attempt to lighten the mood failed as Lyn ploughed on without either responding or looking back at her closest friend.

"It's here." Lyn came to a stop, briefly looking at the weather-beaten headstone, before kneeling into a neatly cut strip of grass that surrounded the grave. "At least there's a record that she actually existed." Lyn leant forward and gently passed her open hand across the inscription:

Amber Burton
A much loved daughter
Lost to all but God

ANT STOOD BEHIND LYN, remaining still as he watched his companion trace each letter with a fingertip. "Strange sort of inscription, don't you think?"

Lyn got to her feet and moved to Ant's side. "Amber may have an epitaph, but she doesn't rest here."

He raised his eyebrows. "Well, this morning proved that, don't you think?"

"Stop it. What I mean is, Amber has never occupied her mother's grave."

Unprepared for her stern rebuke, Ant gazed at the headstone then back at Lyn. "I'm sorry, I didn't mean to—"

"My fault, Ant. I didn't mean to bite. It's just... I mean...
"

He watched as she reached out to the headstone, resting a trembling hand on the wet stone surface. As she turned back to him, Ant was surprised to see a tear trickling down his best friend's cheek.

This isn't like you.

"Come here." Ant held out a welcoming hand. Lyn's tears intensified as she leant into him, his arm now cradling her. "We'll find out what happened to your friend, Lyn. I promise." Lyn didn't respond, but he could feel her nodding as she pressed the side of her face tight against his dripping jacket. "But what about that inscription, Lyn? Amber can't be in two places at the same time?"

Eventually, Lyn pulled away from his calming embrace. "You're right. Amber has never lain here because her body was never found. You were away with the army for years, so there's no reason you could have known what happened."

"So why don't you tell me?" His calming voice caused Lyn's tears to begin flowing again.

She looked back at the headstone. "Amber had it tough at home. Up until her mother died, her father was the life and soul of any party. Then Sarah Burton died suddenly. No one expected it. Amber told me she was having tea with her mum and dad just like they did every day, gossiping and teasing each other as usual. Her mum got up to clear the plates from the table then suddenly collapsed. She died a few days later without ever regaining consciousness. After that, Amber said her father was never the same. He started to drink and developed a vicious temper. Amber reckoned he blamed her for causing her mother's illness because they didn't approve of a boy she was dating. She said to me once that it was almost as if he'd wished she'd have died rather than her mother."

Ant shook his head in disbelief at the revelations. "And all this time you kept it bottled up inside you?"

"You're the one to talk," she snapped.

Lyn had taken him by surprise, such was her flash of anger. Ant held his arms open. This time Lyn resisted his attempt to offer comfort.

Better change the subject.

"So what do you make of the inscription. Remorse?"

Lyn turned her attention back to the headstone. "I guess so. He fell apart after Amber's death and became something of a recluse and refused every offer of help. Eventually the village stopped offering and left the man to his own devices."

Ant raised his gaze to watch the drizzle form a fine mist against the backdrop of the dark solid stonework of the church. "But we now know Amber survived the accident. Was she with anyone?"

Lyn nodded without immediately responding. Ant gave her the time she needed.

"The jet ski was her boyfriend's. She was on the back of it. The weather was awful that day. Why they went out in such rough conditions is anyone's guess. So out of character for Amber. She was always the sensible one."

"Did they both die... I mean disappear?"

Lyn turned to look at Ant. "No, the boyfriend, Jack Spinner, survived but vanished two days after the accident and hasn't been seen or heard of since."

"Convenient, don't you think?"

Lyn gave her friend a puzzled look. "What do you mean?"

Ant moved forward and brushed his hand over the top of the headstone. "Think about it. Amber supposedly drowns, yet her body is never found. Then the boyfriend does a runner?"

She shook her head. "You've been watching too many episodes of *Midsomer Murders*. You know how vicious the tides are around here. Amber could have been dragged out to sea in seconds. As for poor Jack, what would you do, with her father, police, and a couple hundred angry villagers after your blood?"

Ant thought for a few seconds. "Easy, I'd do a runner, except we now know your friend didn't drown that day. What if Jack knew that? What if he rode out beyond Hinchem Point, dropped her off and then faked the accident in full view of the harbour? Did anyone actually see what happened?"

Lyn crossed her arms and hunched her shoulders. "Well, er... as a matter of fact, no. Jack raised the alarm by running into the pub. Apparently, he was hysterical; but then you would be, wouldn't you?"

Ant waved a finger. "Lyn, when needs must, there's a minority of people who can put on a convincing show to convey what they want people to believe. What if they planned it all along? Think about it: if Amber had indeed fallen off in a genuine accident but survived, why didn't she make her way home, or to a friend's house, even your house?"

"What if she hit her head and lost her memory? It happens."

"Yes, but surely she would have been found wandering the streets or in the fields behind the beach; but to simply vanish.... After this morning, I don't believe that for a second. You say she was having problems with her father who, according to you, hated the boyfriend. What if she wanted to get away and never be found?"

Lyn gave Ant a look of horror. "You can't be serious. Why would anyone do that to a parent? It doesn't bear thinking about."

Ant heard the distinctive sound of wet grass being walked through. He turned to see the Reverend Morton approaching. "Something happened to make Amber run. Can you think of anything else?"

Lyn traced a finger across the headstone. "Now you mention it, Amber was distracted by something in the weeks before she... she vanished, but wouldn't tell me, which was unusual because we shared everything."

"Could it have been her father?"

Lyn stared at her friend with an intensity he hadn't seen before.

"I don't think so. She always told me when they argued it was always about Jack. Thinking back now, there was something else. I could sense it. She seemed frightened by something but always changed the subject when I questioned her. Then, again, who knows what goes on behind closed doors?"

"Who's frightened?" The vicar's inquisitive question brought the pair's discussion to a sudden halt. Quickly gathering his thoughts, Ant diverted the reverend's attention.

"Wasps, Vicar, I was just saying I hated the things." Ant waved his arms wildly as if trying to escape a swarm of the insects.

Lyn watched in amused fascination as her friend overacted his part. Nevertheless, the reverend joined in the pantomime. "I, too, hate the things. Once ruined a wedding I was officiating at when one of the blighters stung a member of the congregation just as I was asking if anyone present had any objection to the marriage. The groom almost passed out on hearing a scream, thinking, I imagine, that he was about to marry a bigamist."

The mood changed when Ant informed the vicar why they were in the graveyard.

"Sidney needs to know; I'll go to him now."

Ant placed a hand on the vicar's arm as he turned back to the church. "By the looks of him, he already does."

The three of them turned to see Sidney Burton trudging through a patch of long grass, the lower part of his trousers wet through from the soaking vegetation. "Sidney, may I offer my sincere condolences. Amber now rests in God's kingdom, at peace and without pain." The reverend extended a hand. Sidney Burton ignored the gesture, instead focusing his attention on the headstone that commemorated his wife and only child.

After a few seconds' silence, Sidney turned to Ant and completely blanked Lyn. "The police told me what happened." Tears began to flow as his voice started to break. The floodgates opened as he sank to his knees. "I can't go through this again."

Lyn stood fixed to the spot. It was Ant who offered a comforting arm around his shoulders.

LEAVING THE CEMETERY, Ant stopped at a familiar grave. Standing ramrod straight, he offered a respectful nod before turning towards Lyn who was by now several yards ahead.

"Your brother knows you love and miss him."

Ant gave the faintest of smiles. "I imagine he's looking down on me and thinking to himself how soppy I am."

Lyn reached over to Ant. "Not soppy, Ant. Just a respectful love and nothing wrong with that. Anyway, only I can call you silly names. Anybody else does and I'll have them." She made two fists and began to shadow-box.

"Remind me not to meet you on a dark night, Miss Blackthorn." Ant smiled a contented smile as he wrapped Lyn's petite fists within his large hands. "Now, where do you want to go for lunch?"

Before Lyn had a chance to respond, the beep from a car horn made both of them jump. Turning to see Detective Inspector Riley's police car pulling over, Ant let out a sigh. "What have we done now?"

"Remember, fella, keep your temper."

That's all right for you to say.

The pair watched as Riley clambered out of his car and sauntered up to them.

He looks different.

The detective looked over to Amber's headstone where he could just make out Sidney Burton talking to the vicar. "Poor blighter. No one should have to go through what he's experiencing."

Ant looked at Lyn in disbelief then whispered into her ear. "Do you think he's okay? I think he's coming down with something."

"I think you call it humanity," replied Lyn, adopting her friend's whisper.

Nope, still think he's ill.

"I want to thank you both for this morning. It couldn't have been easy. Especially you, Miss Blackthorn, or may I call you Lyn?"

Blimey.

The confused looks continued between the two friends as Riley forced a smile, making the encounter all the more surreal as far as Ant was concerned. His confusion morphed into curiosity as the detective came to a halt closer to his personal space than the socially accepted metre or so. "Have we transgressed... again, Detective Inspector?"

Riley's forced smile returned. "Not at all, Lord Stanton, or may I call you Anthony? As I said, I genuinely want to thank you both."

Ant picked up on Riley's awkward body language. "And...?"

The detective repeatedly shuffled his balance from one leg to the other. "Well, as you have mentioned it, yes, there is more...." Riley hesitated before continuing. "I, er... It's like this, um. Oh, what the heck. I need your help with this awful drowning."

Ant wasn't sure who was more surprised: Riley, himself, who began shuffling his shoes on the stone pavement slabs, or Lyn, who seemed to have developed a nervous cough. For his part, Ant assumed it was another of the detective's tricks. He studied Riley's face. His nervous twitch had been replaced by the look of someone bearing the woes of the world on their shoulders.

Lyn took the initiative. "I know you weren't working in the village when Amber first disappeared, but you must have read the case file?"

Riley's face flushed as he began to shuffle from one foot to the other again. "That's the problem. I've been gazumped."

"Gazumped? You want our help to buy a house?"

"No, no, er, Lyn... you don't understand. Divisional Commander Paul Lister has gazumped me and taken over the investigation."

Lyn smiled. "Ah, now I understand. You mean he's usurped you." Now it was Ant's turn to cough by way of disguising an involuntary bout of laughter. "That name sounds familiar," she added.

Riley gave Lyn a weary smile. "He was the investigating officer ten years ago. I imagine he interviewed you?"

Lyn thought for a few seconds. "Now I remember; everyone said he was charming. He wasn't with me; I can tell you."

"Charmer or not, it seems he was moved on and promoted shortly after closing the investigation. If ever there was a case of it's who you know, not what you know, Lister is the ultimate case study. When they tried to replace him, no one wanted the job. That's how I finished up here."

Ant succeeded in controlling his urge to rub salt into the

detective's wounds. "How did he hear about Amber's death so quickly? It's only been a few hours."

Riley turned. "Never underestimate the speed at which intelligence moves around Her Majesty's Constabulary. Although Lister is based in Sussex, he has ears like Dumbo and misses nothing. Even so, I don't understand why he pulled rank when he has so much on his plate."

Curiosity aroused, Ant dug deeper. "Perhaps he's worried he missed something during his original investigation, or he's looking to take the glory of finding out what happened to cause Amber's death."

Riley stiffened. "You may be right, but I'm not going to allow him to get away with it. This is my case and I will solve it... er, I mean with the help of Lyn and you, we will succeed."

Ant glanced at Lyn who was returning his grin. He cocked his head to one side and she nodded. "Looks like we're in, Detective Inspector. Let's catch up tomorrow, yes?"

"Excellent, I look forward to catching up with you." Riley hesitated. "Just between us three, agreed?"

Ant smiled. "Don't worry, Detective Inspector. As you say, just between us three."

Riley turned to walk back to his police car. "Well, what do you think about that?"

Lyn slipped a hand between Ant's arm and body. "See, you can keep your temper when you put your mind to it."

"No, I don't mean that, I—"

"I'm teasing. I know exactly what you mean. More to the point, Ant, what in heaven's name is going on between your favourite detective and Commander Lister?"

Ant shook his head as he opened the passenger side door to the Morgan. "I think there's more to this than just tidying up an investigation file. After all, Lister is in a senior position. He doesn't need to get involved with an unexplained death, and if he wanted to drop Riley in it, for reasons we don't yet know, he could do that from Sussex without dirtying his own hands. Very odd, if you ask me, but it'll be all the more interesting to find out, won't it?"

Lyn gave Ant the sort of look she reserved for one of her overexcited pupils. "You really are like a puppy dog. Let's not forget what we were looking at a few hours ago. Remember, Amber is the important one here, not some stupid spat between two men with enough testosterone between them to ignite a box of fireworks."

"What an interesting thought," replied Ant as he shut the car door as Lyn settled into her seat.

He turned the ignition key and pressed hard on the accelerator firing the Morgan into life. Letting the revs settle down Ant closed his eyes as he took in the throaty rumble of the car's exhaust.

"When you're quite ready?"

Lyn's words or, to be more precise, the jab she gave his left thigh with her finger, woke her companion from his motoring ecstasy.

"No need for that. I'm just monitoring if the engine is tuned properly." Ant sensed the look Lyn was giving him without the need to actually see what she was doing. "Yes, all seems to be well; let's be off." A second depression of the accelerator and release of the handbrake saw the vintage Morgan slip effortlessly from the kerbside and leave the church behind to the sound of the clock striking 2 p.m.

"I thought you were taking me to afternoon tea. Why have you turned into High Street?"

Ant hesitated in answering until he pulled up outside the old schoolhouse. "You know the chap we saw at

Sandringham this morning? Well, he wants to catch up for a chat, so I thought I could drop you off at home and—"

"You mean stand me up and avoid opening your wallet... again."

He didn't need to look at Lyn to sense her dissatisfaction. *Now I'm for it.*

4

SECRETS KEPT

Ant was far from happy deceiving Lyn about his meeting. The one thing that had always bound them together was their promise to always be open with one another.

What was I supposed to do after the look she gave me yesterday?

Before he passed through the ornate oak and etched-glass entrance doors of the Northview Hotel, Ant swung around to take in the incredible sea view as the sun licked across the late Saturday afternoon sky. Down at the small harbour that had seen fishermen plying their trade for hundreds of years, he watched as a steady flow of tourists lined up to take a boat tour to a nearby seal colony that made good use of a secluded stretch of shoreline. Turning to his left, a row of tiny shops originally built as fishermen's cottages did a brisk trade in everything from buckets and spades to locally made ice cream. To his right stood a monument to a long-past tragedy at sea serving to remind those who cared to look at just how dangerous the North Sea could be.

Perhaps Amber was its latest victim.

"I didn't think you would come."

The bubbly voice told Ant his companion had arrived. "Jemma, I didn't recognise you out of that heavy raincoat you had on this morning."

The woman, who Ant thought a little younger than him, gave a schoolgirl giggle as she closed the gap between them and planted a kiss on his cheeks.

Steady on.

He could feel himself blushing and not knowing quite how to respond.

"Come on, follow me. I've got us a table by the window, so we need to get a move on before someone else pinches it." With that, Jemma was off, leaving Ant to follow in her wake.

Passing through the spacious bar and into the comfy lounge, Ant pondered how such a big place would survive without the summer tourists. Originally built for middle-class Victorians, who made good use of the newly opened railway which arrived in 1862, the heyday of such visitors had long since gone, and now the coastal village heavily relied on day trippers.

"Here we are, which seat do you want?"

Ant looked at two chairs that sat at forty-five degrees to each other with a copper-topped low table separating them. "Ladies first, I think."

Jemma smiled and chose the sea-facing chair.

I wanted that one.

"Excellent, then I'll sit here, but before that, can I get you a drink?"

Jemma gave him a wide smile, her eyes wide open. "I'm not driving so I'll have a G&T please."

Ant sauntered over to the expansive bar and leant on an

immaculately polished brass pole that ran the full length of the rich mahogany bar front and top.

"May I get you anything, sir?"

Ant smiled at a white-coated waiter whose moustache and hairstyling could have come straight out of Humphrey Bogart's *Casablanca*. "Two afternoon teas plus a G&T and a pint of bitter shandy."

The waiter smiled. "Of course, sir, I will bring your drinks over shortly and pass your food order to the kitchen staff. Table six?"

Ant nodded confirmation as he looked back at Jemma.

She hasn't taken her eyes off me.

He smiled awkwardly as he walked back to table six. "Drinks with tea, sandwiches and cakes to follow." Slumping back into his chair, Ant kept eye contact with Jemma. "Now, what's all this about?"

Jemma looked hurt for a few seconds before breaking into a broad smile. "Tell me about life at Stanton Hall."

The woman doesn't mess about.

"What would you like to know? The Hall's history is well documented, and I'm sure you will have done your research on the estate, and my family. After all, that's what reporters do, isn't it?"

She threw her head back, ran her hands through her long hair, and gave Ant a dazzling smile.

What have I got myself into?

"Yes, I have, but it doesn't tell me what drives you, Anthony, and I've never had afternoon tea with a real Lord of the Realm. Is it okay if I call you Anthony, or would you prefer your official—"

"Er, no, Anthony will do fine, and if you are very good, you can call me Ant. But I thought you might have been more interested in the awful events of this morning?" He smiled as their eyes once again met.

"Oh, I'm sure the police will get to the bottom of it. She isn't the first body to wash up on this stretch of coast and she won't be the last."

Jemma's casual reference to Amber Burton shocked him, though he tried hard not to show it.

She's as hard as nails underneath that girly disguise.

"Well, I suppose that's one way of looking at things, but why so dismissive?"

Ant's words had their effect.

"No, no, on the contrary, I've already filed my piece, but remember the good detective warned me off, so I'm being a good girl. I feel so sorry for that woman. It's no way to meet your end."

Which is the real Jemma Cole?

"Your drinks, madam, sir." The white-coated waiter placed two drinks on the small table with perfection. "Your afternoon teas will be here in fifteen minutes. Is that satisfactory, sir?"

Ant looked up at the man who stood with one hand supporting a silver tray and the other neatly behind his back. "Thank you so much."

The waiter nodded without smiling or making eye contact, then made his way back to his station behind the bar.

"Hmm, I love a well-mixed G&T, and believe me, they always deliver here."

Ant held his pint glass up as a toast to their meeting. "Then you are a frequent visitor here?"

Jemma laughed as she was about to take her first sip of the tall drink. "Hardly. You saw the prices, and my editor has very short arms for his even longer pockets. No, just the occasional treat, but each time I visit, it's exquisite."

A few seconds passed as each savoured their drink, Ant inwardly lamenting he'd had to put up with a shandy rather than a pint of Fen Bodger's pale ale.

"So, you're a military man, Anthony?"

After taking a mouthful of his shandy, Ant carefully placed his glass back onto the table, the condensation on the outside of the glass container making it difficult to handle. "Miss Cole, you know full well I have served. No doubt you also know why I'm no longer an active officer."

Jemma took a long sip of her drink, all the time keeping Ant in her eyeline. "Ah, I'm Miss Cole now. Well, in for a penny, in for a pound. I know you were medically discharged. Why was that?"

Ant's smile subsided. He ran his fingers up and down the glass, its fizzing contents oblivious to the unfolding game. "It's not something I talk about, Jemma. Some things are off limits, even to beautiful, intelligent reporters. Now, where are those afternoon teas." Through luck or good fortune, his timing was spot on. Out of the corner of his eye he noticed a young lady kitted out in the fashion of a Victorian waitress, the hem of her black dress moving gracefully as she walked towards them pushing a delicate wooden trolley holding two towering cake stands, with everything needed for fresh tea balanced precariously on a lower shelf.

"That looks wonderful, don't you think, Jemma? Thank you so much." His words served two purposes, first to thank the waitress for a wonderful service, second, to put Jemma off the scent.

"Er, yes, it certainly does."

Cracked it.

"Come on, dig in." Ant passed a cake stand across to his

companion and placed his own to his right. The table began to resemble a battlefield as it filled with various plates and cutlery, to say nothing of a tea pot, plus various accessories. "Come on, dig in, I'll be mother and pour the tea. Do you take cream, and what about sugar?"

Ant's deliberate strategy of bombarding Jemma with questions and instruction seemed to be working.

That's the way to do it.

However, he hadn't shaken her off completely. "I know what you are doing, my Noble Lord. I—"

"Wrong. I thought you said you had done your homework. Neither my, nor my father's senior title, entitles either of us to sit in the House of Lords. Tut-tut, Miss Cole."

Ant's correction seemed to fall from the reporter's shoulders like snowflakes on a freezing winter's day. "A figure of speech, Lord Stanton. Now, can we dispose of this silly name formality? It's quite irritating."

Ant broke into a broad smile. "You must try the orange fancy. I do love little cream cakes, don't you? I find them quite a tease."

He reacted to Jemma's ladylike laugh with his own roar as he offered the reporter a cake. "I tell you what, Jemma. You keep your eyes and ears open for anything concerning Amber Burton, and I'll arrange for you to visit Stanton Hall to meet my father, do a tour, the full five bob's worth."

Jemma's face lit up. "Are you being serious?"

"That rather depends on whether you come up with the goods, Miss Cole."

"I suppose that why you are an intelligence officer, Anthony."

"I was, Jemma... was."

Sunday morning at Stanton Hall followed its usual routine with breakfast over by nine, Lyn arriving with her weekly cake for Ant's parents, and the two of them strolling around the ancient gardens of the medieval manor to give his elderly parents time for a rest to set them up for the remainder of the day.

The early morning haze had melted away as the sun's warming rays got to work evaporating dew, causing light to distort trees in the middle distance into a shimmering screen where it was difficult to distinguish reality from make-believe. As the two friends walked through the various garden rooms, Ant became aware that Lyn was quieter than usual.

I knew I wouldn't get away with it.

"Mum and Dad loved the Victoria sponge, said it was your best yet."

Waiting for a response, her silence confirmed his worst fears. "Are you all right? What happened to Happy Lyn?"

Ant got more than he bargained for.

"Happy Lyn doesn't like being lied to. Is that enough for you?" She left him standing next to a stand of rose bushes, their perfume filling the Norfolk air with sweet aromas as she turned right, walked at pace through an avenue of pollarded lime trees, and into a secluded spot the family called *the retreat.*

Ant gave Lyn the space he thought she needed before making the short journey through the arch and into a space filled with lavender, planted tight together to form a collection of sweeping curved borders. The only sound breaking an otherwise total silence was a colony of bees going about their business amongst the pungent flowers.

Turning to his left he saw Lyn sitting on an oak garden bench, its colour burned silver after decades surviving bitter winters and scorched summers. Taking his place next to her, he reached out with a hand. She failed to match his token of affection.

"Look, I didn't tell you I was meeting that reporter because I saw the look you two gave each other when she arrived on the beach. I thought it better I didn't mention her again. I was wrong and I apologise." He sensed Lyn relaxing a little as her shoulders dropped by the tiniest amount, and she stopped shuffling a small mound of loose gravel she'd collected between her feet. "Come on, Lyn. I tell you what. I'll treat you to Sunday lunch at the Wherry Inn. What do you think about that?"

She reached out to rest her hand on his, which had now found a home between them on the bench seat. "You certainly know how to charm a girl, I'll give you that. Let's think about it. You lie to me and try to buy me off with roast beef and Yorkshire pudding. You really are a piece of work, Anthony Stanton."

Ant's sense of relief at being forgiven made him more confident than he had a right to feel. "How did you know where I was anyway?"

Lyn smiled, took out her iPhone and tapped one of the apps. "We agreed to exchange *Find My Friend*, remember? In fact, it was your idea so we would always know where the other one was in case we got into a sticky situation."

He felt his cheeks starting to flush.

She's done me up like a Christmas turkey.

"Did you enjoy afternoon tea with her?"

Ant allowed himself a grin, which he worked hard to conceal from his friend.

Do I detect a hint of jealousy?

"And you can wipe that silly grin off your face. You're not off the hook yet. What were you doing in The Smuggler's

Rest until eleven last night? I hear the rooms are quite cheap for a short stay."

I should be so lucky.

"Hold on a minute, Lyn. That stupid app may tell you where I am, but it's not clever enough to tell you *who* I was with. As a matter of fact, it was… well, er, let's just say it was the person I met at Sandringham on Saturday morning."

He sensed the intensity of her look beginning to soften. An emerging grin confirmed his supposition.

Maybe I'm off the hook

"I know that look, Anthony Stanton, so don't think you are in the clear yet. Tell me, was he the man you came out of Sandringham House with? You know, the one who kept scratching his ear. I saw you from one of the museum windows."

Now it was Ant's turn to smile. "Let's just say if you were wearing an earpiece all day, you'd tend to scratch at you ear."

Lyn looked horrified. "Oh, sorry. I didn't realise he was deaf."

Ant let out a roar. "He isn't, but he does work for the Special Branch." Before Lyn could reprimand him again for being too cocky, Ant continued, "Now that we have the conspiracy theories ranging from me having an illicit meeting in a hotel bedroom to spending the evening with a deaf man, can we get on and decide what we do next to find out what really happened to Amber Burton?"

She raised her eyebrows. "Don't push your luck."

Before their exchange could develop further, the Hall's immaculately turned-out butler strode purposefully into the garden of reflection, coming to a halt as soon as he saw Ant. "The Earl requests that you both join him in the library. There is a gentleman he would like you to meet."

The young man left as silently as he had appeared, leaving the two friends to ponder who the stranger might be.

"Unusual for Dad to receive guests in the morning. Come on, it must be something important."

Pulling Lyn gently off the garden bench, Ant led the way, pausing only to allow Lyn to pass though the neat line of lime trees.

"At least you still have some manners, Anthony Stanton."

She's still annoyed with me.

OPENING THE HEAVY OAK-PANELLED DOOR, Ant stood aside to allow Lyn to pass into the snug room with its walls filled with books on all manner of subjects. As he followed her and shut the door behind him, Ant turned to see a stern figure staring back at him from a deeply buttoned wine-coloured leather chair.

They must have emptied a silver mine for all that bling on his uniform.

"Lord Stanton, I wish to talk to you about the body of Amber Burton. I understand you alerted my officers, having disturbed police evidence."

Your officers, indeed. Not even your county, mate.

"And a very pleasant good morning to you, too, Divisional Commander Lister. I trust you are making yourself comfortable in my home?" Ant glanced at Lyn, whom the commander had failed to acknowledge.

"You don't remember me, do you, Commander?"

Lister looked Lyn up and down from his seated position. "I know exactly who you are, Miss Blackthorn. I interviewed you on July 22, 2010. You were, I recall, less than cooperative."

Ant sensed Lyn was about to act and attempted to distract her with the offer of tea from a side table. He failed.

"And I seem to remember you failing to observe even the most basic of manners, never mind compassion. I see your significant promotion has failed to knock the rough edges off you."

Go for it, girl.

Lister's demeanour remained cold and aloof. He toyed with his empty tea cup by rotating it noisily in its saucer.

"Do be careful with the Wedgwood china, Commander. My mother, the Lady Stanton, has a soft spot for rare artefacts."

Lister glanced briefly at the highly decorated delicate cup before ceasing his circular hand movement. "My job is to find out why bodies turn up out of the blue, Miss Blackthorn. I have little time for pleasantries or sympathy." He began to turn the cup again before Ant's raised eyebrow suggested otherwise.

"Ms Blackthorn will do nicely, Commander."

The two exchanged cold stares before the library door slowly opened. A white-haired man poked his head around the heavy door and smiled. "Ah, Commander Lister, I see you have already met my son and his girlfrie— er, closest friend, Lyn."

Lister shot from his chair, stood ramrod straight, and offered the Earl of Stanton a broad smile. "Indeed, I have, My Lord. Your son is a most entertaining host."

Now that's what I call two faced.

"Well, now that we've got the formalities out of the way, shall we sit?"

Ant took the opportunity to once more study Lister's

demeanour. The commander's smile remained fixed, his body language giving the impression of being relaxed.

"Lyn, my darling, sit here next to me. Anthony, I'm sure you can sort yourself out."

Proves where I am in the pecking order!

Lyn gave Ant's father a wide smile as he gave her a peck on each cheek.

"A most wonderful baker, Commander Lister. This young lady troubles herself in providing my wife and I with a most delicious cake each weekend. It's become something of a tradition, would you not agree?"

Lyn blushed as she acknowledged his kind words as she held his hand in hers. "You do know how to embarrass a girl."

For a few seconds all four looked at each other. Ant's father broke an awkward silence. "Now, down to business. I know you will wish my son and Lyn to assist you with your enquiries into that poor girl's death. Isn't that correct, Commander Lister?"

Ant turned his attention to the officer, who was shifting uncomfortably in his chair and felt the need to clear his throat.

"Well, I... er, Lord Stanton, yes, of course. I should welcome any help your son and Miss... er, Ms Blackthorn feel able to offer, but I—"

"Good, that's settled, then. Anthony, is there anything you want to ask the kind commander?"

Ant took the hint and followed up before Lister had a chance to catch his breath. "Thank you so much, Commander. I can't thank you enough for your generous offer. I wonder if you could tell us a little about your original investigation into Amber Burton's accident; that's what you concluded at the time, wasn't it, Commander Lister?"

He watched as Lister flushed. "We had no reason to suspect foul play. You don't need me to tell you how dangerous the waters around here can be."

"Ah, yes, Commander, I forgot that you are yourself an accomplished skipper. I think I'm correct in saying you hold Norfolk Constabulary's speed record for their coastal challenge skiff race?"

Lister pulled his chest in. "Inter-county, actually, and not beaten in six years."

"Bravo," chipped in the Earl of Stanton.

Ant gave a silent clap to complement his father's response. "Quite so, but perhaps you missed something during your original investigation because we now know that Amber didn't die. In fact, she lived for another ten years. What are your thoughts on that?"

Let the game commence.

Lister bristled. "Given the information we had at the time, and having carried out a most thorough investigation, no, I do not think I made any errors. Of course, hindsight is a wonderful thing. I would just ask you to remember that everyone thought the girl had drowned, a theory that stood firm until yesterday."

He can't even bring himself to use Amber's name.

An awkward silence fell for a second time. Once again, it was the Earl of Stanton who ended the stand-off. "Well that's settled, then. I know, Commander, you are a man of your word, and I can rely on you to take whatever steps are necessary to keep these two young people apprised of your investigation and fully informed of developments. In return I am certain they will share any and all information they have. Now, I suspect you have somewhere you have to be?"

It took several seconds for Lister to realise he was being

dismissed. "Er, yes, of course, I have much to do this afternoon. Staffing budgets and so on."

"Then we must not detain you further and thank you so much for sparing us so much of your valuable time. My man will show you out."

On cue, the library door swung gently open to reveal the butler, his left arm pointing, ushering the commander towards the front door.

Sly old fox. You pushed the call button minutes ago.

His father waited for the library door to close before turning to Ant. "Do not trust that man. He has a habit of saying one thing and doing quite another. Be careful, both of you."

5

TWO FACES

Sunday lunch at the Wherry Arms meant getting in early to bag a table. Ant and Lyn arrived first, their friend, Fitch, a few minutes later.

"Ah, there you are. I thought you'd be lunching with the bigwigs at Sandringham House, not eating with the hoi polloi in a pub?"

Ant half closed his eyes and peered at his mechanic friend. "Don't you start. I've had enough leg pulling from that one." He pointed an accusing finger at Lyn, who reacted by adopting a little-girl-lost look. "It's your round, Fitch, and you'd better order three roast dinners while you're at it or we'll be chewing on the beer mats."

Fitch made his way through a throng of people crowded around the bar as Ant settled into a wood-framed chair that had seen better days. "If this thing collapses, I expect a bit of sympathy, not you splitting your sides laughing like last time."

Lyn continued with her look of innocence. "Me? I don't know what you're talking about. I was laughing at the price label on the bottom of those new shoes when your legs flew into the air, that's all."

Ant scrutinised his best friend's expression and concluded he didn't believe one word of her explanation.

"Anyway, you always plop yourself down like an elephant with a weight problem. I've never made a chair disintegrate the way you seem to manage."

Ant huffed and decided to change the subject. "So what do you think of Lister?"

"What does who think of whatshisname?" chipped in Fitch as he returned to the table having caught a fragment of the conversation.

Ant shook his head. "Never mind what's his... I mean Divisional Commander Lister. Have you ordered the food?"

Fitch slumped into his seat, which wobbled from side to side, causing the man to check its construction for soundness.

"You're both as bad as one another."

Fitch looked at Lyn, then Ant, who replied by shrugging his shoulders.

"Jed said they'll be about ten minutes and not to cut it so fine next time." Reaching over, he handed Lyn a Diet Coke before placing a pint of Fen Bodger pale ale in front of Ant, before placing the battered metal tray, complete with beer dreg,s on the floor. Lyn's reaction was to look under the table.

"Don't panic, Lady Muck; the tray's nowhere near you. Ant will cop it if he moves his clumsy feet more than six inches."

Ant shrugged his shoulders again while taking a first gulp of his pale ale. Lyn was less forgiving.

"I'll give you Lady Muck. If you don't behave, you'll be wearing this Coke."

Seconds later Jed made his way to their table with three heaped plates on a wobbly serving trolley.

"All you need is a fancy white headband, black dress and white apron, and you'll look just the job."

The people nearest their table laughed as all eyes fell on the bar manager.

"If you don't wind your neck in, my dear Lord of the Manor, I'll take this lot back and you can make do with nibbling your fingernails."

Ant thought better of responding with a humorous retort for fear of missing out on the best Sunday roast for miles around. "Just joking, Jed. I like your food too much to risk that."

The manager looked at his tormentor, then the food, and once more at Ant. "Flattery will get you nowhere, so you can drop an extra fiver in the charity tin on the bar for your cheek."

"Better do as he says," whispered Fitch. Lyn's harsh look won the day.

"With pleasure, Jed. Now, can we have our food, please?"

Jed's smile broadened. "Of course, sir, my pleasure entirely."

Ant glimpsed Lyn's warning, daring him to bite back and cost all three of them their lunch. "You're too good, Jed. Any chance of some tomato sauce?"

A collective "urgh" cut through the hubbub. "Tomato sauce with roast beef and three veg?" Lyn's disgust mirrored all those who heard Ant's request. "I bet you didn't learn that up at Stanton Hall?"

Ant raised his chin in defiance. "No, but after you've been shot at in the desert all morning, there's nothing better for calming the nerves."

Fitch chipped in, "You mean to tell me you ate this lot in a hundred degrees? I give up."

Ant shook his head and, impatient at being kept from his food, struck the bottom of the newly arrived tomato sauce bottle and squirted its fire-red contents liberally over the roast parsnips, carrots, and potatoes. To make matters worse, he mixed some of the sauce in with the beef gravy that covered the plate and its contents.

"For goodness' sake, Ant, that looks like a crime scene, not food," spluttered Lyn.

The scene calmed as the three of them finally tucked into their meal, stopping only to take a sip of their drinks. Eventually, Fitch's curiosity got the better of him. "So do I get to know who you were talking about when I came back from the bar?"

Lyn recounted their meeting with Lister, and the background that led to his arrival.

"I remember him, two-faced idiot. Do you know when he interviewed me when Amber died for the first time, he was really unpleasant. That was until Father walked in, and what do you know: he turned into Prince Charming. A right bully if ever I saw one."

Lyn nodded in agreement as Ant devoured the last of his lunch. "And you can take it from me, Riley is not a happy chap."

Fitch twitched his nose as he watched Ant soak the remaining mixture of tomato sauce and gravy with a broken bread stick. He turned to Lyn. "And to think he went to public school as a teenager."

Once finished, Ant looked up at his two companions, who continued to stare at him. "What?"

Both shook their heads in disbelief at what they had just witnessed.

"Anyway, my dear master mechanic, what are you up to for the rest of the day?"

Fitch went into panic mode and looked at his wristwatch. "Oh, thank heavens for that. You've just reminded me I've got a car to collect from King's Lynn. Clean forgot about it."

Now it was Ant's turn to squint. "King's Lynn? Who the heck is paying you to tow a car the best part of sixty miles? Do they not have garages out there?"

Fitch offered a contented smile. "Some of us have very loyal customers. Old Mr Sedgworth won't let anyone else touch his Rover, so he pays me to lift, service, and return his car every six months."

Ant looked incredulous. "You mean he's got more money than sense. He must do a huge number of miles for the car to need servicing that often?"

Fitch's smiled widened. "Not really. In fact, he doesn't take the Rover out of his garage if it's raining or the roads are muddy."

Ant threw his hands up. "As I said, more money than sense."

"Anyway, enough about me earning a crust. How are you two going to while away the afternoon, make more trouble for the police?"

"Well, that doesn't take much." Lyn laughed. What do you think, Ant?"

Taking a final gulp of his Fen Bodger pale ale, Ant studied the remnants of froth sliding down the inside of his glass. "I think it's time to pay Sidney Burton a visit to see if there's anything he can tell us about Amber that we don't already know."

He glanced at Lyn, noticing her demeanour had suddenly stiffened.

"Why don't you go on your own, Ant. I've got plenty of schoolwork to be getting on with."

"Schoolwork? It's the summer holidays. You've six weeks to get stuff ready for September, so don't be daft. I want you with me. After all, you know him far better than I do."

Fitch slapped the small round table with the palms of his hands, which made his two companions jump.

"Well, I'll leave you two lovebirds to get on with whatever you decide to do. See you later, playmates."

Neither Ant nor Lyn reacted to Fitch's attempt to lighten the atmosphere. Instead, Lyn sat quietly as she finished off her soft drink and Ant settled the bill.

"Get away from my property."

Sidney Burton's hostility took Ant by complete surprise as the man opened his front door and immediately let loose a tirade of insults at Lyn.

"Whoa, Mr Burton. Please, calm down; there's no need for that kind of behaviour. We've simply called around to see if you are okay and whether we can do anything for you. You know, like villagers do?"

Sidney wasn't listening; his eyes bulged as he started to move towards Lyn.

"I told you this wasn't a good idea. Let's go, Ant." She began to step backwards as Amber's father bore down on her.

"Enough, Mr Burton. Don't take another step. Do you understand?"

Ant's authoritative command stopped the man in his tracks without diminishing the hate in his eyes.

"Anything you can do for me? She did too much for this

family ten years ago when she introduced my Amber to that creature."

Ant looked at Lyn.

"He means Jack Spinner. If I've told him once, I've explained a hundred times that Amber and I went to a dance at the village hall and Jack was there. Neither of us knew him that well, but he took a shine to Amber, and I spent the rest of the evening nursing my lemonade and trying to fend off Jack's bonkers mate. But he won't have it; he's never accepted my explanation."

Sidney began to get agitated again as Ant watched for any sign of movement. Instead, after what seemed an age, Amber's father began to quieten. Eventually, he leant against the door frame and began to quietly weep. As the seconds passed, his distress became a torrent of anguish.

"Here, Mr Burton, let's get you inside."

The man offered no resistance as Ant supported him with an arm under his shoulder and led the distraught father back into the house. Lyn remained rooted to the spot, leaving Ant to tell her to get a move on and help him. Passing from a narrow hallway into the shabby lounge, Ant settled Sidney on a threadbare couch. He looked around for Lyn, who remained at the entrance to the small room.

"For heaven's sake, what's wrong? I know he had a go at you, but let's make at least some allowance for what he's going through, yes?"

Lyn's head was lowered, her body stiff with arms folded tightly across her chest. Ant realised he needed to do more. Checking that Sidney was still, he walked the few paces to where Lyn was stood. "Come on, Lyn. This isn't like you. You've been on the receiving end of worse from irate parents wanting to know why you haven't morphed their precious child into a modern-day Einstein."

Lyn slowly raised her head. Tear-filled eyes told Ant this was more than a reaction to Sidney Burton's behaviour.

"Talk to me, Lyn." He cupped his hand to envelop one side of his friend's face and gently stroked her cheek.

"The last time I was in this room was the night we went to that village dance. He didn't want Amber to go and I almost left, but Amber insisted. The two of them exchanged harsh words. I got to go to a dance with my mate. He never saw his daughter again."

Her tears now fell freely. Ant placed his arms around her and held her gently to him. "Okay, Lyn. I'm sorry. I didn't know, and you never mentioned anything."

She pulled away from him. "You're not the only one fighting demons, Ant. The rest of us have stuff to deal with as well, you know."

Lyn pushed him away and made for the front door. He knew better than to stop the nearest thing he had to a soul-mate. Instead, Ant watched as she hurried from the house and vanished into the narrow passageway that led from Water Street to the high street, and Lyn's home.

He turned to see Sidney Burton staring blankly into space, showing no reaction to what just happened.

"Sidney, is there anything I can do for you?"

Burton ignored Ant's offer. Instead, he began to speak.

"If only we hadn't argued. I could have told her I loved her. I always did that when she left the house. I would kiss her on the forehead, tell her I loved her, and to stay safe. That's what fathers do when their daughter leaves the house, isn't it?"

Ant felt himself beginning to fill up.

Get a grip, man. You've seen and heard far worse than this.

"I don't have a daughter or sister, Sidney, so I can't say how I would react, but—"

"But you have Lyn Blackthorn. I see the way you two look at one another. How would you feel if you argued and then she died without you making up?"

Sidney's words hit Ant like a block of ice. It was something he'd never contemplated even after all the death and suffering he'd witnessed on active duty. A darkness engulfed him. Before he knew what had happened, he found himself driving out of the village as if on automatic pilot.

"FITCH, HAVE YOU SEEN ANT?" Lyn's words spilled down the phone line as she desperately tried to find out what had happened to him.

"No, why, what's happened? I've only just got back from King's Lynn. Do you want me to come around?"

Lyn looked at the phone as if for divine guidance. "No, but thanks for the offer. We were both at Sidney Burton's place. I left without him, and now he's not answering his phone."

"You know what he's like, Lyn, and if he's took off somewhere it's likely there isn't a mobile signal."

Lyn thought for a moment. "No, no, Fitch, you don't know what happened this afternoon. I have to find out what happened. Amber's father got very angry and although Ant calmed him down, who knows what happened after I left. It's all my fault, Fitch. If that man has hurt Ant, I'll never forgive myself."

The phone fell silent. A few seconds later the doorbell rang. Lyn hurried to the front door. It was Fitch. "You know I'm only thirty seconds away and despite what you said, I thought you needed company, young lady."

Fitch's act of kindness set Lyn off. She cried like she'd

not done so since she was a child. Years of pent-up emotions gushed like a tsunami that swept all before it.

"Come here, you silly sausage. Let's get you into the kitchen, and I'll make us a nice mug of coffee." Fitch led Lyn into the large space, sat her down on a wooden stool, and flicked the kettle on. Lyn continued to sob as Fitch looked around for some tissues. "Blow your nose on this."

He handed over a square of kitchen roll and waited. Instead of more tears, she started to smile, then gently laugh. Lyn held out the tissue. "Fitch, it's full of engine oil, or whatever you've been doing in that garage of yours."

Fitch looked on in shame as he realised he hadn't even washed his hands before rushing round to Lyn's place. "But it is best-quality engine oil. I don't use rubbish, you know."

Lyn smiled, threw the screwed-up kitchen roll at him, and wiped her remaining tears away with the cuff of her sleeve.

"That's a bad habit you've picked up from your little people at school." He smiled as he collected the tissue and stuffed it into his heavily soiled coverall.

By now the kettle had boiled, allowing Fitch to make the drinks. As he handed her a mug with two dirty thumb marks around its rim, Lyn peered into the murky liquid.

"You say this is coffee, but what's this black stuff?"

Fitch smiled. "I'm not used to clean mugs. I find them intimidating."

Lyn laughed as she diplomatically placed the oily mug on the kitchen table. "Now I understand why you are still single."

She watched Fitch's confused look before once more trying to contact Ant. As a dozen times before in the previous two hours, the answerphone kicked in. Placing her mobile gently back onto the table, she let out a sigh. "What's happened to him, Fitch?"

"Come on, Lyn, let's not have any more tears. As I see it, we have a few choices. We can call the police, but he's only been off contact for a couple of hours, so they won't take us seriously. I could call on Sidney Burton, but it's highly unlikely he's managed to hurt Ant. I mean, think about it, when the red mist comes down on Ant, I wouldn't rate anyone's chances of getting near him. No. I think we both know where he goes when his PTSD hits him."

Lyn looked at Fitch. "You're right. Why didn't I think of that?"

Fitch smiled. "Because you love him, Lyn."

Lyn glared at Fitch, then scrunched her face as if being presented with the most complex puzzle she'd ever had to solve. Her posture softened.

"I... I..."

"You don't have to explain anything to me, Lyn. Remember, I've known you two since we were kids, and you both got me into trouble for scrumping apples, when it was actually you scallywags that raided Old Brindley's orchard. I saw something then, and I reckon nothing has changed."

"There he is. Now go to him and talk, and I mean talk about stuff."

Lyn clambered out of Fitch's aged Land Rover and walked on the rough ground of the roadside verge towards a blind bend. Looking down the gentle slope, she passed a giant oak tree that bore several deep scars on its weather-beaten bark, grouped in a pattern two feet from the floor. She neared a solitary man sat with his back to her seemingly staring out across the breathtaking landscape, littered with combine harvesters as the farmers gathered in their summer crops. Now she stood quietly behind him taking in that same canvas.

"Hello, you," she said quietly.

"Hello, you," he responded without needing to turn around.

6

FEELING

Three serious-faced planning inspectors stood like egg soldiers in the old stable yard of Stanton Hall as Ant and his architect, Lucas Brennen, arrived.

"Please remember to control your temper, Anthony. Whether you like it or not, the stable yard is covered by the same listed status as the Hall itself. These guys have the power to make or break your application."

Ant shrugged his shoulders. "You mean to tell me that a gaggle of pen-pushers can tell me what I can and can't do on my own land?"

"Don't be so naïve, Anthony. You know perfectly well they can. What on earth is up with you this morning?"

Ant toyed with his car keys as he attempted to put the events of Sunday afternoon to the back of his mind and concentrate on the matter in hand. "Sorry, Lucas, just have a lot going on at the moment."

The architect waved at the three planning officers while whispering to Ant. "Sorry to sound harsh, but forget that now, and concentrate on being nice, okay?"

Within seconds they came within handshaking distance

of the soberly dressed officers. Ant held out his hand to the one who looked to be in charge. The man gave Ant a cursory nod and briefly pressed his hand into Ant's.

So it's going to be like that.

"Lord Stanton. We did agree Monday morning at nine a.m., did we not?"

Ant looked at his watch: it was 9:15 a.m.

"It is important that we get off on the right foot, so may I make it plain that we are a busy department and regard good timekeeping to be the essence of an effective working relationship?"

Ant's blood was up as he listened to the man lecture him.

Yep, it's going to be like that.

Deciding to turn on the charm instead of his natural instinct to throw all three off his father's land, Ant offered a broad smile. "I quite understand, er, I didn't quite catch your names?"

A little of the wind having been blown out of his sails, the officer muttered something Ant couldn't pick up before turning to his colleagues. "Quickly, then, I am Stanley Brown, departmental head for the built environment. To my left is Ms Kelly Jarvis, lead officer for the built environment specialising in construction fabric of historical value. Finally, to my right is Ms Jo Wayland, lead officer for the built environment with special responsibility for habitat and conservation, rare animal species, flora, and fauna."

Blimey, they like their titles.

Ant turned to look at his architect and noted the look he was getting. He winked and pivoted back to his visitors. "Well well. We are an Auguste gathering, are we not?"

Stanley Brown puffed out his chest and fidgeted with his clipboard. The other two offered awkward smiles.

"I suggest we get a move on and get down to business, Lord Stanton. We have your plans, and I note your architect has kindly joined us today. Perhaps you can show us around the stables and talk us through your plans?" Brown gestured in the direction of a now disued stable block.

The next twenty minutes were spent with Ant leading his guests through a series of buildings, some in better condition than others. When required, his architect answered any technical questions the planning team threw up. Finishing where they had started, Ant waiting nervously for their assessment. The two junior officers deferred to Stanley Brown.

"Thank you for spending so much time with us this morning, Lord Stanton, and also to you, Mr Brennen. First of all I would like to say that the council welcomes your plan to provide vocational training facilities for our young people. As you know, we are a long way from the available provision in Great Yarmouth, Norwich, and King's Lynn, so you are ticking the right boxes. However, as you know, we have a complication in that these buildings have a listed status. This means that no changes will be allowed to the exterior of the buildings, but before we get to the construction requirements in terms of materials allowable in any conversion, you will need to carry out a full internal survey and submit the results to my department."

Ant stiffened. "But we have already done that. You are holding the evidence in your hands?"

Brennen glanced at the architectural plans he'd been provided with. "No, you misunderstand, Lord Stanton. You must carry out a bat survey as well as full mapping of any graffiti on interior and exterior surfaces."

Ant gave his architect a look of exasperation. Turning

back to Brennen, he tried to remain calm. "Bats? Graffiti? What are you talking about?"

The planning officer gave each of his colleagues a lofty look. "Lord Stanton. I think a bat survey speaks for itself. They are a protected species, and if they are found in any of the buildings, it is against the law to disturb or move them. As for graffiti, it is the collective term we use for marks or symbols used to ward off evil spirits, carpenters' markings on the roof timbers. In fact, anything that adds to our knowledge of the buildings' past. Of course, we will be happy to arrange for the surveys... at your own cost, naturally."

Ant was about to explode when his mobile sprang to life. Lucas seized the moment. "Anthony, why don't you take the call while I finish off with our guests?"

He took the hint and moved to the stable-block entrance.

As Ant finished his call, he turned to see Lucas and two of the planning officers walking towards him. The third officer hung back, staring intently, as far as Ant could make out, at the tiled roof of the stable block. As the others reached his position, one of them caught his eye.

"How's Lyn these days? I haven't seen her for, oh, it must be ten years." The woman smiled at Ant, her eyes wide as she fixed on his stare.

"Er... you know Lyn? It's Kelly Jarvis, isn't it?"

What's she up to?

She moved closer to him, which in other circumstances he might have found flattering, but there was something about this particular woman that put him on edge.

"Oh, in passing, you know how it is." Kelly Jarvis picked a non-existent speck of dust off Ant's lapel before offering a broad smile and brushing past him, all the time keeping her eyes firmly on him.

A strange woman indeed.

As the stable yard emptied of people, Ant made to make off back to the Hall before remembering one of the planners was still poking around the buildings. He set off to find her. Having popped his head in and out of several buildings, he finally found the woman staring intently at something above an old fireplace in what had been the head groom's accommodation.

"Found something interesting?"

His sudden appearance made the woman jump.

"I'm sorry, I didn't mean to startle you; it's Jo, isn't it?"

She nodded and returned Ant's smile.

Great, a normal human being.

"What was it you were looking at? I'm intrigued."

Jo turned back to the off-white lime-washed wall, its surface flaking after years of being left to its own devices. "See these burn marks on the timber beam above the mantelpiece?"

Ant leant forward to catch sight of where Jo was pointing. "Yes, I see burn marks from the fire, I suppose."

Jo gave a quiet laugh. "Well, you're half right. They are burn marks, but not from the fire."

"Candles," exclaimed Ant, sure that he was onto something.

"Again, half right."

"Come on, Jo, half and half make a whole one, so I must have cracked it."

She laughed again. "If you mean the burn marks are from someone placing the candleholders too close to the wall, you would be wrong. They are known as taper burn marks. Around four hundred years ago when this building was under construction, someone purposely seared scorch marks into the beam. In fact, you find them all over the place, even in places where it would be impossible to situate a candle, and they all have the same distinctive teardrop shape. It's thought they were to ward off lightning. Literally, to fight fire with fire."

Ant raised a hand and ran his fingers over one of the burn marks. "It's quite deep, isn't it? I suppose the amount of timber in medieval buildings meant they were terrified of fire, so I guess it makes sense, sort of."

Jo's smile broadened. "And I bet if you took a proper look in the Hall, you would find dozens of these as well as witches' marks to ward off evil spirits."

Ant turned to Jo. "You really are passionate about this stuff, aren't you?"

"History is so important to us, you know. We must preserve as much evidence as possible so that we increase our knowledge and come to understand our forebears." Jo blushed as she finished speaking.

"No need to be embarrassed, Jo. I love it that you find your subject so fulfilling. I tell you what, if you want, you can look around the Hall sometime and see what you can find. How does that sound?" Ant thought Jo might explode as she took in his offer.

"Do you mean it? That would be wonderful. Such a kind offer."

"Is that a yes, then?"

"It's a double yes. Thank you so much."

His knock on the front door was quieter than was his usual habit. Today was different: it was the day after the afternoon before. He wondered how she was feeling.

"Still in your pyjamas, I see."

Lyn opened the door wider having only popped her head around it until she knew who it was. "Coffee is on. I'll be with you in a minute." Lyn didn't wait for a response, instead leaving her best friend to fend for himself.

By the time Lyn reappeared, two steaming mugs of coffee kept each other company on the large pine table that doubled up as Lyn's workspace.

"I found the last of the chocolate cake. Do you want a piece?"

Lyn shook her head. "What, this near to lunchtime? Did your mother not teach you anything?"

Ant giggled as he cut himself a huge slice of the feather-weight sponge. "It's never not the right time for chocolate cake, Lyn. And, yes, Mother did teach me not to gorge myself, but Nanny Perkins was more forgiving and quite partial to cakes and biscuits herself." His eyes lit up as he took a large bite from his cake.

"Only you could use that as an excuse, Ant, only you."

Once the jovial interlude ended, both sat quietly, each nursing a steaming coffee. Minutes passed as their attention varied from mug to friend and back again. Ant knew it was for him to raise the subject. "Staying in your pyjamas isn't like you, Lyn. Is yesterday still bothering you?"

Lyn concentrated on rotating her mug on the table between her hands. Ant assumed this was to evade his eye contact. He gave her the time she needed.

"Yes... and no." She spoke hesitantly. "It wasn't so much Amber's dad going for me. I half expected that. It was more being in that room. Then you disappeared and I didn't know what had happened to you. That wasn't fair, Ant." She made eye contact to reinforce her point.

Now it was time for Ant to look sheepish. He, too, tinkered with his coffee mug. "The truth is, Lyn, I don't know what happened, or at least I remember Sidney Burton asking me how I would feel if we argued and then you died without us making up. To be honest, I don't remember driving to where you found me."

Lyn reached across the table. Ant released a hand from his mug and gently clasped hers.

"I told you that I spoke with Fitch. He said a couple of things that shocked me. Then he said he knew where to find you. I should have cottoned on but I wasn't thinking straight."

Ant ran his fingers through hers. "I didn't intend to end up where Greg died, at least I don't think I did. I don't know."

Lyn brought her remaining hand over to cover their entwined fingers. "I suppose when we're really down in the dumps, we look for comfort. You seem to find it where your brother died. Does it help with your PTSD too?"

Ant looked deep into Lyn's eyes. She was the only one he truly trusted. "Do you know I call his image up whenever I want, just like I'm talking to you now. Sometimes I ask his advice. Do you think I'm mad?"

"You loved your brother very much, and you still gain comfort from being near him. There's nothing wrong with that. In a way, I envy you."

"And you can't?"

Lyn broke off eye contact. "I don't find it as easy or as comforting as you seem to. As I said, Ant, we all have demons to contend with."

"And what about Fitch?"

"What about Fitch?"

"You told me yesterday he made a comment about how we feel about one another."

"You can say the word, Ant. Or perhaps you can't?"

Ant squeezed her fingers. "What's in a word, Lyn? Does it affect or govern how two people feel about one another?"

Lyn gently withdrew her hand from his and renewed her eye contact. "You know, Ant, sometimes I think men really are from Mars." She stood and walked quickly over to the hallway. "I'll be down in a few minutes."

Ant remained looking at the doorway for some time after Lyn had left.

Now what have I done?

Ten minutes later, Ant heard Lyn's bedroom door closing. Springing into action, he made two fresh coffees and lifted a round cake tin from a wall cupboard and placed it on the table.

"Heavens, you look almost human."

Lyn squinted at Ant. "If you don't behave, I'll put that cake tin away." She closed the gap between them and made for the summer-flower-painted container.

"I'll fight you for it, Lyn."

She made a determined lunge for the tin, which he parried with a gentle swipe of his hand. "Told you I would fight you."

"Give it here." Lyn laughed as she pulled the container from his grasp and made off with it.

Ant quickly caught her and spun Lyn around so that they faced each other, their faces inches apart. "You have a choice, either give me the cake or—"

"Or what, Anthony Stanton?"

Ant gently prised the cake tin from her hand and placed

it on the Welsh dresser to his left. Now nothing stood between them.

"Now that I have the cake, you are off the hook."

Lyn smiled; he could feel her breath on his cheeks.

"What if I don't want to be let off?"

The smiles that they had been exchanging slowly faded to be replaced by an intensity Ant had not felt before. Slowly their faces came closer together until they were almost touching. He watched as Lyn closed her eyes; he followed her lead.

Then his mobile rang. It was if a bolt of lightning had hit them both, and within a split second, Lyn was picking up the cake tin and moving towards the kitchen table, while Ant busied himself pressing the accept key on his phone.

"I thought you'd done a runner again, mate. Where are you?"

"Don't be daft, I'm over at Lyn's."

"I should have expected that. How are the two lovebirds this morning?"

Ant could see Lyn had taken a keen interest in who he was talking to. "It's Fitch." She nodded, then turned her attention back to cutting two slices of cake.

"Don't know what you're talking about, Fitch. Anyway, what's so urgent that I have to interrupt eating my cake?"

"I've heard it described many ways, but never that."

Ant sighed. "What on earth are you talking about? Have you been on the sherry or inhaling too much rubbing alcohol?"

"Don't change the subject. Anyway, since you asked, driving back from King's Lynn yesterday, I had the strangest experience."

Ant laughed. "What you get up to in the privacy of that

battered old Land Rover of yours is of no interest to me, young man."

Lyn giggled even though she couldn't hear Fitch's part of the conversation.

"Oh, very funny. No, I mean I saw someone, or at least I think I saw someone."

"Fitch, there are over sixty million people on these islands. I'm pleased you saw one of them yesterday. Now, if you don't mind, I have a piece of chocolate cake waiting for me." He looked around to see Lyn holding a plate of pure temptation out to him.

"Will you please forget about that stupid cake and listen to me. I was in the pub with Josh Whittaker last night: you know the bloke who—"

"Fitch, I know precisely who Josh Whittaker is, and if you tell me about his run-in with the nuns at Our Blessed Mary convent one more time, I'll put the phone down now."

"For the last time, will you listen? We were arguing about a group called The Spinners. I said they were a skiffle group from Liverpool in the late fifties. Josh said I was talking rubbish and that they were a famous American soul band."

Ant sighed again. "Is there a point to this? If it's any comfort, you are both correct. The Liverpool—"

"Never mind the name of the group... well, I mean not the plural version."

Ant threw his free arm up. "That's it, I've had enough. Time for cake and I'll see you later and if you've any sense, you'll stay off that rubbing alcohol."

Just as he was about to end the call, he caught Fitch calling out a name. "Who did you say?"

Lyn looked on in amused curiosity and gestured for Ant to tell her what was being said.

"Now that's interesting, Fitch. Forget what I said about the rubbing alcohol; you earned a pint, mate. Speak to you later."

He slowly placed the mobile back in his pocket and looked over at Lyn.

"You're not smiling, Ant. What's the matter?"

Ant walked over to his chair, sat down, and took a bite out of his cake. Lyn showed her frustration as he took the time to savour his treat. When he'd finished, he went to pick his cake up again.

"Don't you dare, Anthony Stanton. Now, tell me what Fitch said or I'll tip that plate all over you."

Ant looked at Lyn, then his plate, and back to Lyn.

"He saw Amber's old boyfriend in King's Lynn, yesterday."

7

HOOKED UP

C astle Acre stood proud in its ancient landscape as it continued a centuries-old tradition of offering respite and hospitality to strangers since its heyday as a major East Anglian priory.

"Tell me again why you bought this, will you?" Lyn pointed back at the white Volkswagen camper van conversion as she sat on the remnants of an old flint stone wall, its top worn smooth by many resting travellers over time.

"They're all the rage, these are." Ant stood rooted to the spot as he admired his new purchase. "Think about it: four berths, a sink, fridge and gas hob, not forgetting the electric hook-up, and roof we can raise. Why would you pay for an expensive hotel when you can take your accommodation with you?"

Lyn shook her head and shielded her eyes from the intense sunlight of a Norfolk summer afternoon. "Let me think about that. You say four berths. I say a fold-down seat and a plank of wood up top. You mention the kitchen facilities. I see putrid water being caught in a bucket, a sink so small you couldn't rinse your hands in. As for the fridge, fine if you aren't away for more than three days before it packs in and the frozen sausages turn to mush, and don't get me started on the special camping potty thing, urgh."

"But you are forgetting the electric hook-up."

Lyn gave him a look of pity. "Good point as long as you can find a socket on a soggy campsite in the dark. And as for that roof, how many times have you driven off with the thing still sticking up?"

Ant looked hurt. "You know perfectly well it was just the once, and if that tree had had its lower branches trimmed as it should have, I would have been fine."

"And the power cable you left plugged in? You had people running for their lives as it whiplashed between the pitches, to say nothing of the woman who you lassoed with the thing."

"Yes, yes, you've made your point. In my defence, if she'd been wearing stout footwear instead of those flip-flop things, all would have been well."

Lyn gave him a withering look. "I seem to remember that's not the way her husband saw it. Still, you were lucky to get off with a broken wing mirror. If I'd have been him, I'd have put the windows in."

Ant checked his new wing mirror was firmly attached. "Stop being dramatic. Anyway, do want a cup of coffee or not? And I've got some chocolate éclairs in the fridge."

Lyn stood up and wandered over to the open side door of the camper van and scanned its modest interior. "I hope you brought the proper stuff this time. I've had enough of those little sachets you pinch from the Wherry Arms and stick them in your pocket for months on end. By the way, did you turn the fridge on before we set off?"

Ant now stood by Lyn's left shoulder. "Best discount coffee to be had for a pound. You'll love it. As for the fridge, do you think I'm stupid or something? Of course I turned it—"

Lyn clambered inside and opened the fridge door. The absence of a light told her otherwise. A packet of melted chocolate éclairs provided all the corroboration she needed. "I beg to differ, oh king of all campers in this, your realm." Ant's forlorn look forced Lyn to take pity on him. "Come on, you. Let's get the kettle on. We need something to drink while we lose our dignity trying to eat melted chocolate and runny cream."

Fifteen minutes passed as coffees were brewed and chocolate éclairs half-eaten, with the remainder sliding down various surfaces and pooling on the rubberised floor covering.

"Are you really telling me we have to visit every campsite within ten miles of King's Lynn to check if Jack Spinner is staying on one of them? That's even if he's using his real name, which I very much doubt. It'll be like looking for a needle in a haystack."

Ant let out a chuckle.

"Oh, I'm glad you find it amusing."

"At least we have a needle. We just don't know where it is, but you're right. No use tramping around so many campsites. After all, staying on a site for a few nights is one thing. Digging in for ten years would be incredibly expensive, and he'd have to move from one site to the next on a regular basis, so the site managers would soon spot what was going on. No, I think we should check out a couple of villages around the area Fitch reckoned he saw Amber's boyfriend. Let's start with Hepton-next-the-Sea. Our camper van will look like all the rest, so we should be able to blend in, no problem."

"Even allowing for the wing mirror that's hanging off?"

Ant looked around in alarm.

"Fooled you, King of Campers."

THE NARROW STREETS of Hepton-next-the-Sea was packed with holidaymakers, meaning traffic moved at a snail's pace.

"I think every camper van in Norfolk has descended on the place. This is going to take ages."

British understatement at its best.

"Let's cut up here; I'm sure we can get back to the main road."

Lyn gave Ant a questioning look. "Are you sure?"

"Yes, no problem, that's another advantage of these small camper vans, they can go anywhere a—"

"I don't want to say I told you so, but I told you so."

Ant had managed to get stuck at the top of a tiny cul-de-sac and could move neither forwards nor backwards.

"Now, what do we do?"

He failed to welcome Lyn's statement of the obvious. "If only that bloke in the red Volvo would move a little, we could get around."

Minutes passed until Ant noticed a woman with two small children in his wing mirror, loaded down with buckets and spades, novelty hats, and candy floss big enough to swallow a small child whole. "Come on, come on, you've got to belong to the Volvo." Ant huffed and puffed as the trio wandered left, then right as if they had their pick of any car they wanted. Eventually, Ant realised he'd hit the jackpot. "Yes, yes," he shouted.

Lyn shook her head and checked her seat belt as she realised rescue was at hand. After the customary wave from one driver to the other to acknowledge a good deed, Ant revved the engine of the camper van, swung hard on the steering wheel and completed a perfect three-point turn. Ten minutes later, they were back where they had started on the main road, only this time heading out instead of in.

"Let's call in this garage; they'll know all the local gossip."

Lyn put her hand up to stop Ant in his tracks, much like she did with unruly little ones at school. "Mine will be a Twister. You can choose whichever ice cream you want, but remember what your mother said about needing to lose weight."

Ant tutted as he acknowledged his orders.

After what seemed like an age, Ant returned with Lyn's treat and his own low-fat tub. He found the sight of the village head teacher licking an ice lolly, as if her life depended on it, slightly odd.

"What?" said Lyn as she spied him watching her. "Mind your own business and get on with you... what, in fact, is it?"

Ant glanced at the tiny cardboard tub and little plastic spoon he was holding. "Apparently, it only contains eighty calories."

Lyn studied the container. "There's more cardboard than there is ice cream. Still, thinking about it, you'll be gulping more fresh air, which doesn't contain any calories at all, so well done."

He didn't find her analysis helpful and spent the next thirty seconds scooping out the meagre contents with his finger, since the plastic spoon gave up at the first attempt.

"Come on, you were in there long enough. That old chap must have said something of interest, or I wouldn't have got my ice lolly; I know you, remember."

Ant finished off the last of his treat, checking one last time that no ice cream had escaped his attention. "You know it's funny. It was only when I mentioned Fitch that I got anywhere. It seems he has quite a following in these parts, which bamboozles me, but it takes all sorts, I suppose."

Lyn looked exasperated. "Information, good companion, information, please?"

"Well, it seems Fitch called in here after he thought he saw Amber's boyfriend and asked around, something Fitch spectacularly failed to mention when he rang me this morning. Anyway, it seems there's a bloke who has a small cottage off the beaten track. He says it's at the bottom of somewhere called Lane Ends. Apparently, it's a dead end. I guess thinking about it, the name sort of gives it away."

Lyn smiled. "Then let's get to it. Onward to Lane Ends, James." She stretched out her arm and pointed a finger to emphasise her point.

"Hold your horses, impatient one. Although this chap apparently keeps himself to himself, it doesn't extend to the lady he lives with."

Lyn could hardly contain her excitement. "Is it possible they are—"

She fell silent. Ant guessed why. "We need to rationalise this as something that can really push our investigation on. Amber's gone, Lyn. If it was Jack that the man the garage owner saw occasionally, then he will be in one of two states. Either he'll have done a runner because he killed Amber, or he'll be in hiding because he expects to be next. Sorry to sound so cold, but that's the truth of the matter."

Lyn nodded, her facial features sullen. "That means you're certain Amber was murdered, rather than killed in a boating accident?"

"The more I think about what's gone on and, in particular, the sudden arrival of Commander Lister throwing his weight around, my gut feeling tells me there's more to this than a simple accident. It doesn't change things for poor Amber, but if I'm right, it does mean we have a chance of finding her killer. That, at least, will be some form of closure for her father so that he can finally grieve for his daughter."

Newly invigorated, Ant fired up the camper van and made his way to where the old man had said he thought the stranger lived. Lyn studied a Norfolk road map, which she had recovered from the door pocket.

"Two roundabouts, then first left, I reckon, Ant."

"That ties in with what the old chap said. Keep your eyes peeled."

Lyn counted down the roundabouts and kept her eyes open for a small opening on her left. "Turn here, that's Lane Ends."

Ant struggled to see where she was pointing. All he saw was a thick stand of trees stretching far into the distance that formed the road boundary. He slammed on the brakes without checking if any vehicles were following. The sound of a horn told him he was in bad books with the driver of a car he'd probably almost given a heart attack.

"Good job. I thought you'd have us in the trees for a few seconds."

Not half as relieved as me.

As they left the main road, the daylight morphed into a twilight world that was neither day nor night such was the density of the trees, which also formed a near-closed canopy over the road.

"We seem to have left all civilisation behind, Lyn. If you're going to hide, I guess you do it properly."

Both peered out of the front window of the camper van as they strained to see much more than fifty feet in front of them as the slim road narrowed to a track, which appeared to come to a dead end. Bringing the van to a halt, Ant climbed out. Shortly after, Lyn followed. They stood in the middle of the track and looked back from where they'd come from.

"I bet this is a creepy place at night."

"Ant, this is a creepy place now, never mind when the witching hour arrives."

Ant offered a faint smile as he attempted to hide his frustration. "That guy was adamant 'the stranger' as he called him, lived at the end of this road. I guess he must have been mistaken. We'd better get back to the main road and try a bit farther down."

Realising Lyn hadn't responded, he turned to where she had been stood. Now he stood alone with no trace of where his friend remained.

"Lyn," he shouted. "Lyn," he shouted again, his voice raised to its maximum.

"All right, don't shout."

Lyn's reappearance behind him did nothing for his nerves.

"Look over here." Lyn pointed to a felled tree running in line with the track.

"It's a tree trunk, and a big one at that, Lyn."

She smiled, walked over to the tree, and gently pressed with the sole of her shoe.

"Good grief, it's moving." Ant couldn't hide his surprise.

"Look around the back. It's hollow but you would never guess that from the road. Very clever, don't you think?"

Ant did as Lyn suggested. "Well, blow me down, beats any of the camouflage stuff we used in the army. But it might just be a coincidence. For it to be of any use, it needs to be hiding something." He glanced over at Lyn, who was gesturing to him a few feet farther into the thicket.

"And so it does. Abracadabra." She gently pivoted to

what looked like a solid wall of vegetation. In fact, it was a hazel hurdle covered with vegetation. The effect was to completely hide its true function.

"If you're right, Lyn, we should find our cottage a little deeper into the forest. In fact, I'd say just about, there." He pointed to a spot where the light was brighter than its natural surroundings. Thirty seconds later they left the dankness of the thick forest canopy and stood in a small clearing in the middle of which was a chocolate-box farm-hand's cottage.

"You would never know it was here, and we're only about fifty feet from the track."

"You're right, Lyn, but it can't have been a picnic living here. Think about it, you'd have to change the vegetation on that hazel hurdle every three or four days or the dying leaves would be a right giveaway. Not just that, you would have to change with the seasons. No mean feat."

Lyn concentrated her attention on the cottage. "And living in that would be none too comfy. I bet there's no gas or electric or inside loo. Then, again, if you wanted to disappear, it's the price you pay."

"I agree, Lyn, and the genius thing is that because the building isn't connected to any services; no meter readings, no inspections. And I bet it doesn't appear on the council list as requiring tax to be paid. In fact, I'd go as far as to say where the utility companies and council are concerned, this place is listed as not fit for human habitation. Perfect, wouldn't you say?"

Lyn nodded as she stepped forward to take a closer look.

"Steady, Lyn. We don't know if anyone is inside, and if they've gone as far to hide their presence as we think they have, they are hardly likely to offer us a cup of tea and a garibaldi, are they?"

They exchanged glances and instinctively knew what to do. Ant peeled off to the left, while Lyn turned to her right.

"Anything?" asked Ant as they met at the back of the tiny property.

"Not a breadcrumb to say anyone has lived here for ages."

"Let's search the outhouses; see what we can find."

Lyn followed Ant's instruction. Each investigated one of the broken-down constructions.

"Nothing in here, Ant. You?"

He appeared with a lump of coal. "Whoever lives, or did live, in this place knew what they were about."

Lyn gave him a puzzled look. "But it's coal?"

Ant smiled as he inspected the lump of black material more closely. "Yes, but why would you go to the expense of buying coal when the cottage is surrounded with fuel?" Ant pointed at the trees. "Then again, this isn't any old coal. It's smokeless fuel. Now, isn't that just genius."

Lyn's eyes lit up. "Of course, damp timber would act as a smoke signal to say someone lived here."

"Exactly, Lyn, whereas this stuff burns clean and does what it says on the tin: no smoke."

The crack of a tree branch brought their conversation to a screeching halt. Each looked in the direction they thought the sound came from.

"From over there, I think," whispered Lyn.

"No, over there," replied Ant. "Either way there's nothing for us here; we'd better get moving."

Within two minutes, both were back in the camper van. Ant kept the engine revs low to avoid excessive engine noise giving them away. After another of Ant's textbook three-point turns, he gently let the clutch and pressed the accelerator pedal with the lightest of touches so that the van was almost silent as it made its way back up the track to the main road.

"Ant, what are you doing?" Lyn's alarmed cry caught him off guard.

"What, oh... I've got it."

Lyn's alert had saved them from Ant driving the van into one of the hundreds of trees that lined the track.

"What were you thinking of?"

"I, er—"

"You what? Never do that to me again, Anthony Stanton. What were you looking at?"

Ant looked over at Lyn, who was still gripping the handle above the passenger door, her knuckles white such was her purchase.

"There was a man watching us, and I think I know who it was."

8

RELUCTANT FRIENDS

"So let me get this straight. You almost killed us in that stupid camper van of yours yesterday because you think you saw someone who you think you recognised?"

Ant hesitated before answering as he navigated a tricky crossroad on the edge of Stanton Parva and turned left for the run to King's Lynn. "Well, having slept on the matter, I'm now of the view that it wasn't so much a definitive identification; more a sort of, likely. Don't worry, it'll come to me in a day or two."

Tuesday promised to continue the hot weather of the previous week as the late morning sun moved lazily across Norfolk's big sky. Picking up the A148, Ant allowed his Morgan its head and sped through miles of open countryside, interspersed with picture-postcard hamlets and small villages that nestled into the landscape as if one had been created at the same time as the other.

"Remind me again why you're dragging me all the way out here just to meet that doe-eyed reporter; what's her name? Oh yes, Jemima."

Ant tutted. "Lyn Blackthorn, you know perfectly well that her name is Jemma Cole, so stop being catty; it doesn't suit you. If you must know, she left a message for me at the Hall to say she had some important information she wanted to share." He looked across to see Lyn picking at her nail varnish.

"What?"

"You only do that when you're in a stinker of a mood. Come on, out with it, what have I done to deserve the nail treatment?"

Checking her hair was still in place as the increasing speed of the open-topped Morgan caused a rush of wind into the cockpit, Lyn stopped picking at her nails and placed both hands onto her lap. "All we've been doing since Saturday morning is rushing around, chasing our tails without getting anywhere, Ant. Poor Amber is lying on a gurney in the cottage hospital morgue, and we are no nearer to finding out what happened than we were when you turned over that little boat on the beach."

Ant wanted to bite back, but there was more to Lyn's mood than her words. He slowed the Morgan down and brought it to a stop on a patch of ground that bordered the road.

"Why have you stopped?"

"Because, Lyn Blackthorn, we need to talk." Ant twisted to his left so that he faced Lyn head-on. She, on the other hand, kept her gaze firmly on the pure black carpet in the passenger well. "We can't change the fact that Amber is dead any more than we can turn the clock back to have stopped your friend from going to that village dance ten years ago. But think of the progress we've made since we found Amber. We know she didn't die all that time ago, and we are fairly certain she's been in hiding with her boyfriend.

Plus, we know something spooked her in the run-up to her original disappearance."

Lyn shot Ant a cold stare. "But we don't know how she came to be on that beach. We've no idea what she was afraid of to make her run... and her father still hates my guts." She reached for the door handle, yanked it hard, and climbed out of the Morgan.

He could see the effect going over old ground was having on his closest friend. Ant found dealing with her raw emotions a difficult conundrum to solve. All he could do was tell her the truth as he saw it. He leant across, stretching his hand out to rest on the passenger seat to support him. "You're right, there's a great deal we don't yet know, but one thing is for certain, if we can find Jack Spinner, we'll be a long way down the road to solving what happened ten years ago and what led to Amber's death on Saturday. Now, do we get on with this, or hang around here theorising about what we do and do not know?" Ant took his hand from the passenger seat and held it out to Lyn. The beginnings of a smile gave him encouragement. "Come on, let's go and meet your favourite newspaper reporter."

She opened the car door and wafted his outstretched hand away.

That's my Lyn.

"LOVELY TO SEE YOU AGAIN. Lyndsey? At least we don't have a body this time."

Oh no. Here we go.

"And wonderful to see you again, Jemima."

This is not going to go well.

"Well, that's the pleasantries over, you two. Now, lead on, Jemma. We are in your hands."

I wish she would stop smiling at me like that.

The reporter led her guests through the busy open office of the King's Lynn Clarion, which was filled with the sound of computer keyboards clicking noisily as reporters toiled to file their stories before the copy deadline. Leading her guests around a far corner, she showed Ant and Lyn into a tiny office next to a huge shredding machine.

"I don't know why we have that because journalists never throw anything away. Now, here we are; take a chair and make yourselves comfortable."

Jemma's guests looked at each other as they scanned the tiny space that somehow managed to accommodate a desk, typing chair, and two metal-framed plastic seats.

"It's a bit mucky," Lyn whispered to Ant.

"Reminds me of a teenager's bedroom," observed Ant.

Two minutes passed as the pair amused themselves by counting the cobwebs before Jemma reappeared holding a strip of old wood twelve inches long and three inches wide, on which three vending machine plastic cups made a valiant effort to stay upright.

"Anyone for sugar?" Jemma tossed half a dozen paper sachets onto her cluttered desk. "Don't use the stuff myself, rots the teeth, you know."

Ant avoided looking at Lyn since he knew if eye contact was established, both would break into laughter.

"That's so kind of you, Jemima. No sugar for me; as you say, it rots things."

Behave, Lyn.

"Looks great, thanks, Jemma." He caught a glance from Lyn. Her look said it all.

"My pleasure," replied Jemma, studiously avoiding Lyn's presence.

A few seconds' silence followed as Jemma took several sips from her plastic cup, stopping occasionally and placing the drink on her desk to give her fingers a chance to cool down. Lyn, on the other hand, spent her time peering into the murky liquid, eventually deciding the best course of action was to put the container to one side. Ant fiddled with two paper sachets of sugar, spilling more on the floor than into his cup.

"So, Jemma, you have some important information for us?"

The reporter smiled. "Yes, I have. However, I am a reporter, so what do I get in return?"

Ant could see Lyn fidgeting in her chair and guessed what might happen if he failed to control the situation. Placing his coffee on the floor and taking the opportunity to blow on his fingers, Ant clapped his hands and let out a throaty laugh.

I hope this works.

Ant's reaction startled both women. Lyn gave him daggers; Jemma almost spilled her coffee.

"Well, that's not quite the reaction I was expecting and it's not often us old hacks find ourselves surprised."

"I'm amazed you're surprised at anything, Jemima. We are talking about the death of a young woman after all."

Ant looked on helplessly as his companions exchanged smiles through gritted teeth.

"And, of course, someone to whom Lyn was very close." His look pleaded with the reporter to soften her approach.

"I'm sorry, Lyndsey, I wasn't thinking. Please forgive me."

It wasn't quite the approach Ant wanted Jemma to take, but at least he hoped it stopped Lyn going for the reporter.

"As you say, Jemima. Of course, cognitively speaking, 'thinking' is regarded as a high-level function. Some of us exhibit more of this trait than others."

Not that scary grin again.

"You know, ladies, I feel like a referee failing miserably to control two cage fighters. Can we get back to why we're meeting?" The silence that followed, together with two pairs of eyes burning into him, told Ant he'd done something wrong. He could not, for the life of him, determine what it was.

"Don't you dare call me 'lady,'" said Jemma sternly.

"I agree with her, don't mess with the sisterhood."

I give up.

Feeling bruised by the encounter, Ant tried a more businesslike approach, deciding it was the safer option. "Jemma, Lyn, I apologise unreservedly. Now, if I might suggest we get back to why we're here in the first place?"

Honour satisfied, Lyn went back to scowling at Jemma, who completely ignored her and, instead, tapped her computer keyboard to bring the screen back to life. Ant watched as she studied an email.

"Now, where were we, oh yes, you were about to tell me what I get in return for giving you the information I mentioned."

And who said men were the tough ones.

Ant fixed his eyes on Jemma's, hoping she would break first. She didn't. This wasn't something he was used to. "Look, what about afternoon tea at Stanton Hall. My father, the butler, the silver service... and I'll throw in a guided tour."

I may as well throw the Hall's door open.

Jemma smiled, pushed a key on her laptop, and looked over to the printer. "You have a deal. Have a look at this."

She handed the still-warm paper from her laser printer over to Ant. Several seconds passed as he studied it, leaning into Lyn so that she, too, could digest its contents.

"Can you trust your source?"

Jemma broke into a broad smile. "Look at the email address at the top. Recognise the surname?"

Ant followed her advice. "Ah, I see. Brother?"

The reporter laughed out loud. "My father. He's been a fisherman for decades and knows the local tides like the back of his hand. Give him a local weather forecast, and he'll let you know exactly how the tide will be doing four hours from now."

Lyn relieved Ant of the email printout. "So your dad is saying the boat Amber was found in couldn't have travelled far given the intensity of the storm?"

Ant watched with interest to see if Jemma would look at Lyn directly. Instead, she kept her eyes on him.

"And there's more. I rang Dad after getting his email and pinged him a picture of the boat. Well, he recognised it straight away as an old wreck that had been tied to a harbour stake two hundred yards up the beach for months."

Ant frowned. "Amber could still have taken it."

Jemma turned back to her computer and pressed a second key. A detailed map of the local coastline snapped into view. She pointed at the screen. "Dad says that given the seas were being driven by storm-force onshore winds, there's no way anyone, let alone an amateur, would have got more than a few yards in that little boat without being tossed out of the thing."

Lyn folded the email and slid it into her jacket. "Then how did the boat end up on the beach?"

Again, Jemma addressed her answer to Ant. "Someone trying to control a heaving boat in a storm is one thing. An empty boat having broken loose from its mooring is quite another. Dad reckons that given the swell on Friday night, which he says was about ten feet, and the wind direction, that boat would have been picked up like a matchstick and thrown yards up the beach."

Ant and Lyn looked at one another, concern for Amber etched on their faces.

"That means Amber was murdered?"

"It looks that way, Lyn." He turned to Jemma. "I take it you won't be releasing any of this stuff?"

"I'm a reporter; what do you expect me to do?"

Ant stiffened. "I'm Lord Stanton who is a gatekeeper to the Earl of Stanton, and the silver service."

Jemma sat back in her threadbare computer chair. "That's not fair."

Ant's face remained fixed. "Neither is being found murdered under an old boat."

For the first time in an hour, Ant observed Lyn smiling.

"So you haven't told anyone else, Jemma?"

The reporter winked at Ant. "Not even that nice Commander Lister. Funnily enough all he wanted to know was if I had anything on... what's his name, that Jack Spinner chap."

This new information set Ant's mind racing.

What's going on here?

Lyn broke her silence again. "And do you have any information about Jack?"

Jemma looked at Lyn for the first time that afternoon. "No, I checked the archives, both online and hard copy, and, other than a reference to him disappearing after his girlfriend died in a boating accident, I drew a blank."

Lyn's body language softened. "Did you tell Lister that?"

Good question, Lyn.

Jemma gave her adversary a cold stare. "As a matter of fact, I didn't. I told him I'd have a look and get back to him. I haven't done that... yet."

ANT SLIPPED on his sunglasses as the Morgan headed into the sun on the way back from King's Lynn. "Am I glad to be out of there. She's crackers."

Lyn didn't respond as she rummaged in the passenger glovebox.

"What are you muttering about?"

Eventually she retrieved her sunglasses and gave Ant a cold stare before putting them on. "For someone who prides himself on conserving vintage cars, you're a mucky pup when it comes to the bits people can't see."

He shook his head as if bemused by her assertion. "I said I'm—"

"I know what you said. As far as I could make out, you were quite enjoying the attention the doe-eyed one was giving you. Perhaps I should start wearing eyelashes long enough to plait."

She turned to face him. He turned towards her. All either could see was their own reflection because of the polarised lenses they were wearing.

It's like a scene from The Blues Brothers.

"Don't be daft. As I said, the woman is crackers. Anyway, she's not my type."

Lyn took her glasses off so that he could properly gauge her expression. "And your type would be...?"

Is that a trick question?

Ant hesitated. "Preferably seventy-five years old with a

straight-six-engine configuration and stainless-steel, spoked wheels." He decided to keep his eyes on the road.

"Stupid man."

The pair settled into a few minutes of quiet as the Morgan ate up the tarmac and hedgerows whizzed by, their progress slowed only by an occasional tourist taking the narrow bends far too fast for Ant's liking.

As another car appeared out of nowhere, Ant shouted and shook his fist. "Crazy driver, you could have killed us all."

Lyn took off her glasses again and shot him one of her special head-teacher looks. "Kettle, black, pot. Please rearrange to solve the puzzle."

He shook his head and thought better of taking Lyn on. "So where are we up to? A body on a beach, seemingly no sign of injury, yet we're told she couldn't have drowned. A boyfriend who also disappeared years ago and appears to have done a runner for the second time."

"He might be dead."

Lyn's stark intervention startled him. "Why do you say that?"

She removed her sunglasses and was about to start cleaning the lenses with a tissue from the centre console, before thinking better of the idea on seeing what was on the tissue. "I hate men."

Ant shrugged his shoulders. "So what's new? On the floor, there's a new packet. Don't worry, they haven't been opened."

Lyn felt under the passenger seat, eventually retrieving a surprisingly clean packet of tissues.

"What if he was next?"

Ant lowered his head trying to find scarce shade from the

burning sun. "That presupposes he didn't kill Amber himself. As I've said before, who knows what goes on behind closed doors. Imagine being in hiding for ten years with little money and seemingly no way to change things. That would put a strain on the strongest of relationships, don't you think?"

Lyn nodded. "You know, that's been puzzling me too. Why didn't they move away? Why stay within forty miles of where you apparently drowned? They were taking a heck of a risk of being discovered."

"Fool," Ant shouted at yet another tourist taking in the sights instead of keeping their eyes on the road. "You make a good point, Lyn, but what if Amber just couldn't bring herself to leave her father? Perhaps a guilt thing, who knows?"

Lyn placed the sunglasses back on her head. "I suppose that makes sense, but if you're right, they were in danger of—"

"Of what?" Ant interrupted.

Lyn fell silent for a few seconds. "Amber was running from something, or more likely, someone. I don't know whether it was Jack Spinner, in which case he found her, and they made up; her father... or someone else. The problem is, Ant, questions are coming thick and fast, but making any sense of it all seems to be running away from us like a beach ball in a howling gale."

Quiet fell again as the Morgan reached the outskirts of Stanton Parva.

"Talking about things that howl, we'd better bring Riley up to date. I can't believe I'm saying this, but I do feel sorry for him."

Lyn smiled. "Now that's a first. But you're right. Why don't you ring him first thing in the morning?"

As Ant brought his car to a stop in front of Lyn's place,

he suddenly remembered something. "Oh, by the way, I forgot to tell you. I met one of your old friends yesterday. Now, what was her name?"

"I don't know, Ant, that's what you were going to tell me."

"Very funny. She asked after you and seemed very friendly, but a bit scary at the same time if you know what I mean?"

Lyn shook her head and began opening the passenger door. "No, Ant, I don't, and if it's okay with you, I just want a few hours quiet after the day we've had."

"Kerry. Yes, that's it, Kerry something or other. She said to give you her best wishes. He watched as Lyn froze. "What on earth is the matter; are you going to faint?"

She stood rooted to the spot.

"You mean Kelly Jarvis." Lyn's voice started to tremble.

"What on earth is the matter?"

Lyn leant against the side of the Morgan.

"Kelly Jarvis was one of the most jealous girls I ever came across. She had a big thing for Jack Spinner. When Amber hooked up with him, she threatened to..."

9

IN THE CELLS

After completing his usual ride around Stanton Estate on his quad bike, Ant parked the vehicle up in the Hall's garage complex and sauntered back into the great house. As he chatted to one of the house staff at the bottom of a magnificent oak Jacobean staircase in the hallway, the butler appeared.

"Mr Anthony, you asked that I remind you to ring Detective Inspector Riley. You mentioned that it was important."

The prompt hit Ant like a bolt of lightning; there had been so much going on, it had gone out of his head. "What would we do without you, David?"

Rushing into the morning room, Ant flicked open his mobile and hit the auto-dial key. After listening to the line ring out for several seconds, he was about to end the call when he realised it had connected and a whispery voice floated into his ear. "Is that you, Detective Inspector Riley?"

"Shush, someone might hear you."

"Are you feeling unwell, Inspector?"

"Keep your voice down, will you? Hang on while I find somewhere where no one can hear us."

Ant's bewilderment grew as the line went silent. A few seconds later, the whispering recommenced.

"That's better, can you hear me, Lord... er, Anthony?"

He's finally gone mad.

"Yes, but you sound as if you're in an empty box. Where are you exactly?"

A moment's hesitation followed.

"If you must know, I'm in the cleaner's cupboard. We won't be disturbed here. Not by the cleaner anyway, he's a lazy mongrel."

Perhaps it's a nervous breakdown.

"I hesitate to ask this, but why are you whispering... and why are you hiding in a cupboard. What's wrong with your office?"

Once again, a moment of silence descended.

"I've been evicted from it by Lister. He's pulled rank and told me to find somewhere else to work from."

"And you picked the cleaner's cupboard?"

Ant listened to Riley mutter for several seconds without catching anything the man had said. "What did you say, Inspector?"

"I said the only free space I could find was one of the cells."

Ant roared with laughter as he conjured up a mental image of the detective having messages and his tea and favourite biscuits served through the cell door hatch by a bemused constable.

"It's not funny, you know. The seat in there is as hard as stone; in fact, it is stone. And I can't see out the window without standing on top of the toilet bowl."

By now Ant was almost wetting himself. It was almost too much to take in.

How the mighty doth fall.

"I still don't get you hiding in the cupboard. Do you like being in the dark?"

Ant was sure he heard Riley swear.

"Because Lister is watching every move I make, and that of my officers. The man's paranoid. He won't let anyone in his... I mean, my, office, and he's had all the files from Amber Burton's case dug out from the archives. My desk sergeant says Lister has the lot under lock and key. Anyway, the cleaner doesn't work on a Wednesday. Actually, he doesn't work most days, but on a Wednesday he's not physically on the premises."

Ant almost collapsed in a fit of giggles.

"Anyway, what do you have? I assume you have information for me, or am I your entertainment for the day?"

Ant finally managed to compose himself. "As a matter of fact, I have several things and we need to meet. I'd rather it wasn't in the cleaner's cupboard if you don't mind. I'm allergic to bleach and damp mops."

Ant thought he'd caught Riley swearing again.

"Ha, ha, very funny. Listen, I have the perfect place. Meet me at that café on the Norwich Road, the one with all those little statues out front, but be careful, the goons Lister brought with him will be all over the place looking for me once they find out I've left the station."

Lister brought his own staff: interesting.

"You mean There's Gno Place Like Gnome?"

"What?"

"There's Gno Place Like Gnome. That's what the café is called.

"Whatever."

"How about twelve o'clock? I'll treat you to a sausage butty."

A moment's quiet fell before Riley responded. "Make it

twelve thirty and hold the sausage. I hate pork. In fact, I hate pigs. Vicious things, they are."

Ant cried laughing at the image Riley painted.

"Are you still there? What's that noise? Are you in a cupboard too?"

Ant could take no more. It was all he could do to splutter acceptance of Riley's revised timetable.

Lyn will never believe this.

"IN A CUPBOARD?"

Ant delighted in recounting his conversation with Riley as Lyn powered her MINI Clubman along a variety of meandering country lanes before reaching the old Norwich to London coaching road.

"I just wish I could have been a fly on the wall for that conversation. Anyway, why do you think he picked that particular café to meet. It's not exactly local, is it?"

Ant looked thoughtful as he tried to fold his long legs into a comfortable position. "I imagine because it stands on what counts as high ground and you can see for miles around. He said Lister was paranoid. If you ask me, they make a right pair."

Lyn laughed. "High ground? There isn't much in Norfolk that's more than a hundred feet above sea level."

"I agree, but it does stand atop one of the few inclines you'd be out of breath pedalling up on a bicycle."

"Fair point, Ant."

Twenty minutes later, Lyn's MINI slowed as she pulled off Norwich Road and into the car park of the café, leaving a dust cloud rising behind the car from the hardened clay surface.

"Are we early, or Riley late?"

Ant looked at his watch. "Spot on twelve thirty."

Both car doors opened within a second of each other as the two friends surveyed their surroundings.

"They are a bit spooky, aren't they? Look at that one with the fishing rod. I swear he winked at me." Lyn pointed to a brightly painted stone figure twelve inches high in a crouching position, his diminutive fishing rod and line dangling into an ornamental pond, which contained a variety of plastic wildlife including a pair of flamingos that seemed to have fallen out with each other, assorted otters, and a one-eyed hedgehog.

"And I swear that hedgehog twitched its nose at me," replied Ant. "Ah, speaking of wildlife, look, I spy Riley's car tucked behind that hedge. Ant pointed to a line of hawthorn hedging in dire need of a trim.

"Yes, I see it. Well, you did say Lister had made him a bit twitchy."

"Twitchy is one way of putting it," replied Ant as he led the way to the café's front entrance and pushed the door open. "Looks empty, Lyn. I guess the gnomes have had their lunch and are back, er, doing whatever it is that gnomes do."

Lyn smiled as she looked around the relatively small interior, complete with gingham curtains, half a dozen small square tables, and yet more gnomes in various guises on every surface. "It's very spooky. No wonder the place is empty."

"Psst."

The two friends instinctively looked to see where the odd sound came from, then turned their attention to each other. Both shrugged their shoulders.

"Psst."

Ant smiled as he spotted the tips of two brown brogues

sticking out from under a floor-to-ceiling gingham curtain screen.

Only he *still wears those things.*

"It's not like the inspector to be late: he's usually such a diligent fellow."

Lyn gave her friend a curious look before catching onto his game. "I know what you mean, Anthony. Let's hope no harm has come to Inspector Riley. I've grown quite fond of him lately. Shall we ring the police station?"

A stifled cough and the sound of chair legs scraping the floor like fingernails on a chalkboard filled the air. "Psst, for heaven's sake, it's me."

Adopting a surprised look and trying not to overact, Ant and Lyn watched as Riley's head appeared around a curtain in the far corner of the room.

"Oh, you're safe, Detective Inspector Riley. We've been so worried about you, haven't we, Lyn?"

She placed a hand to her heart and gave an exaggerated sigh. "Oh yes, very worried indeed, and to think you were ensconced there all the time."

Ant gave Lyn a strained look as both realised that she'd meant to say concealed.

Riley poked his head out a little farther, like a tortoise stretching for a piece of lettuce. "Never mind that now. Come behind the curtain so no one can see us."

They were just about to make the short journey when a familiar voice rang out.

"I can see you. In fact, I can also see my empty cash till since you've only had one cup of tea in the last forty-five minutes and not so much as a chocolate doughnut."

The stout woman winked at Ant and Lyn.

Riley disappeared back behind the partition to escape

the establishment owner's onslaught, much to the amusement of the others.

"I see you have lost none of your charm. Lyn, meet
Patience Ploughwright. How's things?"

Patience smiled as she placed a hand on each ample hip
and displayed a matching pair of Cromer crabs, one on each
bulging forearm to match her pink hair.

"Oh, you know, up and down. It's fine in the summer
with all the tourists, like. But it's quieter than a graveyard
full of relatives who've fallen out with each other, in the
winter months. Still, I have Horace for company."

Ant smiled, "Ah, so Horace is still with you?"

"Knows he's onto a good thing, that lad. Gets all the food
he can eat, and he can't half eat, then sleeps for most of the
day."

"Sounds an ideal existence, Patience." Ant laughed.

The proprietor picked her nose with a stubby finger and
expertly flicked the results into the air, before inspecting her
cuticles to ensure no trace of the organic material remained
attached to her pink-coloured nail. "Got to keep your hands
clean, you know, health and safety and all that."

"Psst."

"Anthony, either I've got a gas leak, or One-Cup Charlie
is calling you."

Ant raised his eyebrows. "I think your gas pipes are quite
sound, Patience. And to make up for the good inspector's
lack of spending power, bring us three full English, will you?
Hold off the bacon and sausage on one of them and plenty
of fried bread and mushrooms. Oh, and keep the tea
coming, will you?"

Patience's smiled broadened. "You've just made Horace's
day. Okay, be back in twenty minutes."

Lyn was already waiting for Ant at a small table tucked

behind the gingham curtain screen. Ant took his seat, pulled the curtain back to allow light to penetrate the otherwise dark corner, and fixed his gaze on the detective.

He looks like death warmed up.

Riley's anxious look intensified as the glass frontage of the café illuminated the clandestine gathering.

"Don't panic, Inspector, better to see who's coming than guess from behind a curtain, yes?"

"Anyway, it's good to get a bit of air circulating. It feels like a turquoise bath tucked in this corner."

Both men gave Lyn a strange look.

"I think you mean Turkish bath, Lyn."

"That's what I said?"

"No, Lyn, you definitely sai—"

"Said Turkish. Why would I say turquoise?"

Ant sighed and pondered whether to push the point. He decided he was in the right. "Tell me, what colour have you been banging on about painting that pine panelling in your bathroom? I don't suppose it would be Turkish, would it?"

Lyn scrunched up her eyes, her nose twitching. "Now, who's being silly? You know very well it will be turquoise."

Ant smiled knowingly. "I rest my case."

"Should I leave, or was there a purpose in meeting you two this morning, other than to debate the difference between interior design or men with oily hands pummelling punters?"

Riley's intervention broke the impasse, though the two combatants continued to give each other the occasional sly glance.

"So you're saying Amber Burton is unlikely to have drowned; you think she may have been murdered? And what about the man you thought you saw down the track? Have you had any further thoughts on him?"

Ant shook his head. "As I told you, he looked familiar, but I just can't place him. Now, if I may ask you a question: how do you think Lister will go about his investigations?"

Riley laughed. "Not particularly thoroughly from what I've heard. The man is hated in the Sussex force. I've not managed to find anyone below my rank who has a good word to say about him."

Ant scratched his chin, deep in thought. "And what about ten years ago?"

Riley frowned. "Only my desk sergeant was here then, and he wasn't directly involved in the investigation. He did say he got the feeling Lucas wanted the case shut down as quickly as possible. It seems he brought in an expert on coastal tides and came to the conclusion Amber had been washed out to sea, so that was that. The coroner agreed with the findings Lister put in front of her and determined it was death by accidental drowning."

"And after?" Lyn chipped in.

"Lister, you mean. Well, from what I can gather, he didn't hang around. In fact, he was promoted within the year, and since then, his elevation in the Sussex force seems to have been nothing less than meteoric. Seems he's known down there as Teflon Shoulders because nothing ever sticks to him."

"Do you think he'll pull the same trick again?" asked Ant.

"That's what's puzzling me. If he'd have stayed out of it, he could have deflected any criticism of his actions ten years ago by arguing the coroner hadn't disputed his findings.

Would you believe she congratulated him on the sensitive way in which he'd carried out his investigation!"

Lyn gasped, "What, Lister?"

"Well, we know he can be charming when he wants to be. You said it yourself up at the Hall the other day, Lyn."

"You're correct. When he's on public show, there's no one better at pulling the wool. In private it's quite another matter. Anyway, back to my main point. Given he decided to poke his nose in it begs the question, why?"

Riley's companions looked at one another, then back at the detective.

"What if he's trying to find something. Something he missed all that time ago," suggested Lyn.

Riley licked his bottom lip. "Or trying to hide something. It's an interesting conundrum, don't you think?"

Ant turned back to Riley. "As you say, Inspector. Well, you know everything that we know now. Any advice on what we should do next?"

Riley placed a hand in the inside pocket of his light-weight jacket. "If I were still on this case, I'd want to interview anyone who was on that beach, plus those living along the clifftop within two hundred feet of where you found Amber Burton."

He handed Ant a single sheet of paper that had been tightly folded into three. "I took the liberty of making such a list. Lister has not seen this, but he's sure to have had something similar compiled. All I would say is, be very careful. The police officers he brought with him have, how shall I put this, something of a reputation for taking shortcuts. Short hair, big fists, you get the idea? So be—"

Ant noticed Riley literally freeze at the same instant he heard the distant sound of a police siren piercing an otherwise peaceful environment. At that moment, Patience reappeared from the kitchen holding three immense plates of food, one in each hand, and the third expertly balanced on one of her tattooed forearms.

The sound of the police cars got louder. In seconds, a cloud of dust was thrown up as several sets of raging tyres formed what looked like a sandstorm about to engulf the café.

"Our friend won't have time for his food, Patience. Can you help?"

She flicked her head to one side, indicating Riley's exit route. "Through the kitchen and take the second door on the left. That will lead you into the old air-raid shelter. Shut the shelter door behind you and no one will get in. Just watch out for Horace, fella. He doesn't like his sleep being disturbed."

Riley sprang to his feet and shot past Patience. "Don't worry, I won't disturb your husband. I'm specially trained in covert operations." In seconds he was gone.

Lyn turned to see Ant in hysterics. Patience had tears streaming down her face. "Am I missing something here?"

Patience wiped her eyes, leaving black streaks from handling overcooked mushrooms.

"I wonder if he's been specially trained in avoiding bad-tempered pigs?"

10

THE LIST

"Well, it sounds as if you two have been busy." Ant's father grinned at both of them as he handed each a cup of Earl Grey tea. "Now, make yourself comfortable and tell your dear mother and me what you've been up to."

Lyn settled herself next to Ant's mother, while he sat opposite his father as he explained who and what they had seen and their conclusions.

"So not an accident, son?"

"That's what we think. The problem is for every question we answer, at least another two pop up." Ant felt a gentle hand on his lap.

"Your father and I know Lyn, and you will get to the bottom of it. I am sure of that."

He smiled as he looked deep into his mother's eyes, which as far as Ant was concerned, had never lost their sparkle.

I do love you, Mum.

"I think you have more confidence in our deductive powers than Lyn and me."

Lyn chided her best friend. "You speak for yourself. I'm with your mum."

"I think you're outnumbered, son," chipped in his father "Now, who's for the last of Lyn's excellent cake?"

Ant glanced at the cake stand and noted there were two slices left.

A hint, I think.

"Mum, would you like a piece?"

He caught Lyn giving him a look of mild chastisement.

She's doing it again.

"Yes, of course you would, Mum. Here, let me get it for you."

He watched his father smile as Ant handed the cake to his mother, then focused his attention on the last remaining slice.

"And I know you would wish me to have this, son."

Lyn giggled as Ant saw his final chance to snaffle the cake disappear into his father's open mouth.

Ant decided to rationalise his loss by focusing on the investigation. "The odd thing is that Commander Lister's name, or influence, keeps popping up. Can you tell Lyn and me anything about his background that might help us make sense of things?"

The Earl of Stanton finished his cake and placed a fine bone china plate onto the rounded oak coffee table that rested between them all. Wiping the remains of any crumbs from around his mouth with a delicate white cotton napkin, he fixed his gaze on Lyn, then Ant. "To answer your question back to front, I can tell you his ultimate undoing will be his raw ambition. You both saw it on open display when we met him the other day. Would I be correct in thinking he was less forthcoming to you two than the deference he showed me?"

Ant smiled. "But you are the Earl of Stanton; that's not an unusual reaction, is it?"

"On one level, no. But Lister has a particular way of paying attention to those he thinks can be of use to him. Others in my circle have made the same observation. I had quite forgotten his modus operandi until he reappeared the other day."

Ant scratched his head. "I see that, but not sure how that helps us."

His father held a finger up. "But don't you see? If you use his faux charm against him, you are certain to catch him out and he will make a mistake. Now, I do not know what he's up to, but from what you've told me, he's not suddenly reappeared after ten years because he has a hankering for the Norfolk Broads, no matter how mesmerising they are."

Lyn leant forward. "Gerald, I have my own memories of the man and, looking back, can see how he persuaded people to do what he wanted. What is it, other than his ambition that makes him tick. There must be more to the man than that?"

The Earl of Stanton looked over to his wife who had started to nod off in her chair, smiled, then turned back to Lyn. "Anne caught onto him immediately. She said he'd learned to hide his emotions for fear people would think him weak. You have to understand, Lyn, Lister is what might euphemistically be called an alpha male. In his mind, he can't afford to be seen to have any flaws, hence the charm he uses to deflect difficult situations."

"Some say charm, others might say deception," chipped in Ant.

"Very true, but the important question is, what made him like he is?"

"You mean the nature, nurture thing, Gerald?"

"Exactly, Lyn. My view, for what's it's worth, is when it comes to Lister, it's very much the former. His father was a senior officer, you know. I imagine he drilled ambition into his son. My guess is Lister learned early on to do whatever it took to prove himself to his father. One classic way of doing that is to always be in control—control people, information, and resources. That way he always gets what he wants. His genius is to charm those he needs something from."

Ant picked up on the theme. "So is there a flip side to this man."

His father nodded. "As there is with every one of us, Anthony. In Lister's case I think it is the failure of his marriage. When he worked here, I believe he still lived in Cambridge. Now that's a heck of a commute every day, and, added to the odd work patterns of police officers, and particularly detectives, it took its toll on the relationship with his wife and son. From what I can remember, she left him around the time that young lady you found on Saturday first went missing."

Ant looked shocked. "Wife? Did you ever meet her?"

"Only from afar; he would occasionally bring her over for community police do's, you know the sort of thing. She seemed very nice. Anyway, I suppose it was Lister's attempt to involve his wife. Didn't work, though, she left him shortly before your young lady vanished. I imagine that for such a vain man who expected to be able to control events, it made him very angry."

Ant and Lyn exchanged concerned glances. "Do you think it could have made him so angry that he did something that ten years later he needed to make sure no one found out about?"

Ant's dad put a conspiratorial finger to his nose. "I know this much, Lister's father did time for corruption and causing actual bodily harm, and prison is the last place a serving policeman wants to end up. Deduce from that what you will."

WEDNESDAY EVENING in Stanton Parva's Wherry Inn was normally a haven of tranquility, sitting as it did between hectic weekends of summer tourists and thirsty locals. This evening was different.

"If I've told you once, Fred, you've had enough to drink. Go home and have some food, sober up, and come back later. If you're in a fit state, I'll let you have one more pint." The bar manager, Jed, pulled himself up to his full six foot two and nineteen stones to tower over the sixty-two-year-old farmhand.

"I'm as sober as a judge and, you, Mr Ful... ller, Fillu... ler, Fuma... lly, Jed, have no right to keep a man from his beer."

"Go on, Jed, let the man have another drink; this is good fun."

The bar manager turned to the heckler. "And you'll be next out the door, and see what your Irene thinks of having you under her feet all night."

The bar erupted into laughter as the heckler broke off eye contact with Jed and buried his head in his pint.

"Come on, Fred, home you go." It wasn't a request this time as Jed lifted the inebriated man from his bar stool and guided him out of the pub just as Ant, Lyn, and Fitch were trying to get in.

"Another one bites the dust, eh?" Ant laughed.

"If you go on at this rate, you won't have any punters left, Jed," added Fitch.

"You be careful on your way home, Fred. There's still plenty of cars about, so stick to the path. You hear me?"

Fred offered Lyn a smart salute to acknowledge her order before weaving his way down High Street and making good use of a line of lamp posts as jumping-off points from one safe haven to the next.

"Inside, you three; my bar's looking a bit lonely tonight, and the till has forgotten how to open."

The three friends needed no further encouragement to enter the establishment, and as they entered the cosy bar, they were greeted by assorted hands waving and the odd "evenin'" from the small assemblage.

"Sit you down, I'll bring them over," said Jed as he disappeared behind the bar.

"Nothing like being predicable, is there?" Fitch laughed.

"If it means I get my Fen Bodger all the quicker, I'll settle for that."

Ant didn't have long to wait, and soon the small bar table was filled with three glasses of alcohol.

"Tell you what, I'd loved to have seen Riley's face when he found out Horace was a pig, and a bad tempered one at that."

The other two laughed, risking spilling their drinks.

"I hope he escaped in one piece. Can you imagine the headline: 'Pig Caught with Snout in Policeman.'"

Lyn shook her head. "Anthony Stanton, you are cruel. What if he really did get hurt?"

Ant gave her a mischievous smile. "Well, he did say he hated bacon. I imagine he hurt Horace's feelings, so he probably got what he deserved."

The three friends broke into laughter before each lifting their glass.

"To pig lovers everywhere, and may the force be with them," shouted Ant.

A minute's comparative quiet followed as thirsts were quenched. Fitch was first off the mark.

"And you say Riley gave you a list?"

His two friends were taken aback by the sudden change in the direction of the conversation.

Ant gestured to Lyn, who reached into her shoulder bag. "Yes, but it's just a list of names and contact numbers that Riley had his officers collect from people on the beach and surrounding area. I'm not sure what good it will do because I imagine they saw what we saw, but the good detective was keen that we follow them up."

Fitch took the single sheet of paper from Lyn, placed it on the table between their three drinks, and smoothed out its surface so that he could get a clear look at the names. Seconds went by in silence as he slid a finger from one name to the next.

"You're being unusually studious, Fitch," said Ant, bored of waiting.

Fitch lifted his finger from the list before tapping one name in particular and slowly looked up. "This one might be worth looking at. If it's the same man, I've come across him before."

"Do we really have to do this tonight, Ant? It's a fair old way back to Sidbourne Deep, and I've got stuff I need to do at home, you know, like washing and ironing." She looked at Ant as he released the handbrake of the Morgan and propelled the car forward. "Oh, silly me, of course housework is not something you have to concern yourself with, is it?"

"Meow," said Ant, without taking his eyes off the road.

Lyn hit the gear lever, causing the engine to scream in protest as the car started to glide in neutral. Ant immediately pressed the clutch and put the car back into gear. "Are you crazy? You could have killed us."

Lyn smiled. "Well, at least I'd have got your attention."

An uneasy stand-off descended for a few minutes as each glared at one another, Ant making sure they were still on the correct side of the road.

"What's the harm, Lyn? Riley made it clear that he fully expected Lister to have compiled a similar list. Doesn't it make sense to get at some of them first, especially now that Fitch has given us the heads-up on that bloke?"

She flipped the vanity mirror down and checked her lipstick, tidying one corner up with the edge of a paper tissue. "All Fitch said was that the guy's name reminded him of someone he knew in the area who was a bit of a scallywag."

"So?"

"So it's a huge jump from being a bit of a chancer to murdering a woman, don't you think?"

Ant increased speed as they hit the main road to Sidbourne Deep. "You're right, Lyn. But he was there on that beach, yes, just like all the others, but what if, and I know it's a long shot, but what if he did have something to do with Amber's death, and we failed to at least talk to him?"

Didn't mean that to sound so hard.

Lyn went quiet and sank back into the leather-covered passenger seat of the vintage car.

"Look, I'm sorry, Lyn, I didn't mean to—"

"No... no, you're right, I'm wrong. Of course we have to check the man out. It's just..." Her voice tailed off.

Ant slowed the Morgan so he could make himself heard a little easier. "But you're right, too, Lyn. Perhaps it will be a wild goose chase. I tell you what, when we're done, why don't we nip into King's Lynn for a meal. I'm paying."

She flicked the vanity mirror back into place and shot him a wry smile. "And will it be just us two, or will the delightful Jemima be joining us?"

Ant put his foot on the accelerator, causing the vintage car to spring to life. "Just us two... and you know perfectly well her name is Jemma."

Lyn grunted and placed a hand on her hair in an attempt to impose at least a vestige of control over her hair as it flailed in the wind of the open-topped Morgan.

"THERE'S NO ONE IN, Ant. Look, it's a house on its own in the middle of nowhere with at least two days' worth of newspapers sticking out the letter box. We're wasting our time here."

Walking up the long, narrow pathway from the quiet country road to the front of the lime-washed cottage, Ant scrutinised every inch of the scene for signs of life. "You may be correct, Lyn, but let's just spend a couple of minutes looking around."

The two friends made their way down one side of the old building before arriving at a side gate.

"We can't go through it, Ant; that would be breaking and entering. Do you really want to spend a night in the cells? Because I don't. I want that meal you promised me."

Ant looked around as if half expecting someone to jump out at him. "Don't worry, listen."

He put a cupped hand to his ear.

"I don't hear anything?"

"Precisely my point, Lyn. It's as quiet as the grave around here. You keep your eyes peeled on the road and watch for strangers. I'll check out the back garden."

Lyn turned to walk a few yards down the pathway to get a clear view of their surroundings.

A few seconds later, Lyn heard a man's scream, followed by the terrifying sound of snarling dogs. She looked around to see Ant flying down the path, closely pursued by two Staffordshire bull terriers.

"Run, run for it. They're after blood."

Instead of panicking, Lyn stood firm. "Hold."

Suddenly the barking stopped. Ant stopped running and looked back to see Lyn patting one of the dogs, with the other licking her arm vying for attention. Continuing to keep his distance, he whispered to Lyn, "What are you doing? Let's get back into the car before they have us for supper."

The sound of Ant's voice set the dogs off again, and it was only Lyn's repeated command that saved the day.

I've had enough of this.

Two minutes later, Lyn joined Ant in the Morgan, having secured the dogs back into the rear garden. "You are a wuss. Call yourself a soldier. Heaven knows how you managed in the desert."

Ant lifted his chin, adopting a superior stance. "All they had was AK-47s, not the teeth of a shredding machine and jaws like the gates of hell."

Lyn continued to give Ant a look of derision as he put his seat belt on, checked there were no raging dogs near the car, and made a quick exit back onto the main road to Sidbourne Deep.

———

"THIS IS THE LAST ONE, Ant. I'm not knocking on any more doors to be told I have no right to be selling double glazing at this time of night and shouldn't I be at home with my children, and that was only the women, for heaven's sake."

Ant laughed as he headed through what constituted Sidbourne's town centre and out the other side. "At least they talked to you. One bloke half opened his front door and stuck his walking stick out at me. Yup, they're a friendly lot around here."

Erupting into laughter, the old friends spent the next few minutes seeing who could mimic their assorted assailants the best. The mood changed as the Morgan neared a small car park, which allowed access to Sidbourne Deep beach.

"Do we have to? Why don't we just go for our meal?"

Ant caught hold of Lyn's hand as they walked towards where they'd found Amber's body.

"Two minutes, Lyn, just two minutes. Perhaps we'll see something we missed on Saturday."

"But, Ant, it's going dark. What can we possibly see in the dark that we couldn't see in broad daylight?"

Ant suddenly stopped, causing Lyn to be pulled backwards since they were still holding hands.

"Well, there's one thing that's easy to see at this time of day."

Lyn looked at Ant, then to where he was pointing. House lights, of course. Do we know if they are on Riley's list?"

"Only one way to find out, come on."

The two friends ran back to the car park and up a small track which traced its way along the top of the cliff. In minutes they stood looking at the front door of a large stone cottage standing in splendid isolation and without boundary fences of any kind. A solitary light shone from a downstairs room.

"Your turn, Ant, I'm not being harangued by any more women. You can take your chance with any walking sticks that come your way."

Ant shrugged his shoulders, knowing when he was beaten. He started towards an old-fashioned front door, the top third of which contained an opaque leaded scene of a boat being tossed around on an angry sea.

"And watch out for any dogs."

He looked back towards Lyn, not altogether sure if she was joking. He gave two hesitant knocks on the weather-beaten wood, which reverberated around the hallway beyond. Suddenly a porch light he hadn't noticed illuminated the scene, causing Ant to jump back in surprise.

"Remember those dogs."

"Do you want that meal or not, Lyn Blackthorn?"

Before Lyn could reply, the front door creaked as it started to open. An elderly woman stuck her head out. "What do you want? If you don't shift, I'll set the cat on you."

Her threat confused Ant for a few seconds, assuming she meant dogs. Then he caught sight of the largest cat he'd ever seen, which hissed and spat with such venom that he decided to take two steps back.

Time for a bit of guile, I think.

"Please, madam, I had no intention to alarm you, but I wanted to ask if you saw anything odd on Saturday morning. You will be aware that a young woman was found dead at the foot of the cliffs a little way down the track there."

The old woman stuck a slippered foot across the cat to dissuade it from attacking. "Who wants to know?"

Ant smiled and bent forward slightly as if offering a polite bow. "Of course, madam, how uncivil of me. My name is Anthony. Lord Anthony Stanton."

The elderly lady lifted the cat off the floor with her foot and encouraged the animal to vacate the scene. It did so after offering Ant one last hiss.

"Lord Stanton, you say. Then what is your father's title and what is his wife's first name?"

The woman's questions startled Ant, but he figured this was progress. "Well, my father's title is Earl of Stanton and my mother's first name is Anne. Are they known to you?"

The woman's eyes narrowed. "I mean his family name?"

She's a sharp one.

"Ah, I understand. Our family name is Norton-D'Arcy."

His response acted like the password to Ali Baba's cave. Instantly the old woman opened the front door to its full extent, allowing Ant to see an interior that didn't seem to have been decorated since WWII.

"Your mother was very kind to me some years ago, and I assume you are made of the same stuff, so out with it. What do you want to know?"

Ant turned and gestured for Lyn to come forward.

"Ah, this is your young lady, is it?"

Ant smiled. He could feel himself blushing. Lyn broke the awkward silence.

"The woman found on the beach on Saturday was an old friend of ours. We just want to know if anyone saw anything odd, or out of place."

The old woman studied both their faces. "Yes, I can see you are telling me the truth, and you are Lord Stanton, I suppose." Her eyes fell on Ant. "If you must know, I'm sick and tired of people trespassing on my land. Just because there aren't any fences, every Tom, Dick, and Harry think they can tramp all over my land. Do you know, some of them actually look through my windows. They don't half shift when I set my cat on them, I can tell you."

Ant and Lyn let out a joint laugh as an automatic response to the old lady's talk of her cat.

"Yes, quite right, too. Did you see anyone in particular on Saturday morning? I was on the beach, and I'm sure I saw a man with binoculars standing somewhere up around here?"

The elderly lady bridled. "Oh, him, Monica soon got rid of him. He ran like a scared rabbit when I let her out."

Ant looked past the old lady to the end of the hallway where he noticed the cat loitering with intent.

"Ah, Monica, a fitting name. So he ran for it. Have you seen him since?"

The old lady's eyes flashed. "He won't be around here again. Next time Monica will have him. To be honest, I was surprised he came back so soon."

Ant's ears pricked up. "You'd seen him before?"

The elderly lady leant forward as if about to leak a state secret. "Oh yes, he was here the night before. It was blowing a gale and raining. Monica hates the rain and didn't want to see him off; I bribed her with a dead pigeon I'd found that morning."

Ant and Lyn exchanged excited looks.

"Could you describe him to us?"

"Not really, I left it to Monica. But the girl he was with was a pretty thing."

11

A DOG'S LIFE

I t had been some time since *Field Surfer*, the Earl of Stanton's vintage wherry boat, had plied the Norfolk Broads, which was why he'd asked Ant and Lyn to take the vessel, once a common site in East Anglia as a working boat, for a run.

"It's good to be on the Broads again. Your dad got lucky when he found her."

Ant untied a final mooring rope and gently pushed the wherry from the grass bank. "He often says it was love at first sight, which Mum always teases him about, but remember, it took him years to turn what was essentially a rotted wreck into the fantastic thing it is now. He never says anything, but I guess he's sad he and Mum don't feel confident enough to sail her anymore."

The bright early morning sun glistened off the gently rippling water as *Field Surfer* caught a gentle breeze to assist her stately progress across the gentle landscape of northeast Norfolk. A kingfisher, perching on a mooring post, watched as the boat passed by, waiting for calm to return so that it could get on with the business of fishing.

Rounding a gentle curve, the wherry sat peacefully in the water as marginal vegetation moved rhythmically from side to side as if waving good morning to all who passed.

"It's a world away from what we've been up to since Saturday. Do you think your dad had an ulterior motive?"

Ant gestured for Lyn to pull the tiller a little to the right so they were in the correct position to navigate a low bridge just ahead. "You know Dad. He's always at least two steps ahead of everyone else, so perhaps he could see we were both getting a bit frazzled."

Lyn gently repositioned the wherry's tiller as Ant pivoted the mast through ninety degrees to allow the boat safe passage beneath the ancient crossing.

"And do you think we get too close to things, Ant?"

Standing up from a crouching position after successfully transiting the bridge, Ant turned to Lyn. "I guess it's almost impossible not to, especially when, like in this case, one or both of us knows the victim. We'd be pretty cold fish if we didn't feel at least something." He could see his answer hadn't fully addressed Lyn's concern.

"But do you think we jump to conclusions too quickly? Take last night as an example. The old lady says she saw a man with an attractive woman, and suddenly we think they are in some way involved in Amber's death. Perhaps they were just young lovers getting a bit of space from their parents. It doesn't mean they are killers, does it? Then there's Jack Spinner. We've convinced ourselves he must be in hiding, yet we have absolutely no evidence. Are we so obsessed with wanting to prove someone hurt Amber that anyone who even vaguely fits our view of the crime is fair game?"

Ant waved to a couple passing in the opposite direction in one of the dozens of day-hire boats that plied the Broads during the tourist season. "You might be right, Lyn, but we both know it's worked for us in the past. Just think of poor Burt Bampton. If it had been left to Detective Riley, his death would have been put down to a tragic accident. It was only because we dug away to find out what really happened that we proved he'd been murdered. I guess what I'm trying to say is it's good to be passionate, to stick with something when others think we're being awkward. There's a lot to be said for gut feeling, Lyn."

She returned his warm smile and allowed her head to tilt backwards so that she caught the full glory of the warm morning sun.

"Er, never mind the sun, watch what you're doing with that tiller or you'll have us against the bank."

Lyn overreacted to Ant's instruction, for which he earned one of her head-teacher looks of disapproval.

"I might have known 'nice Ant' wouldn't stick around for long. Anyway, skipper the thing yourself if you think you can do a better job."

Ant wagged a finger. "I'll remember that the next time you criticise my driving."

The ping of a message arriving to his mobile distracted Ant from discussing his driving abilities further. "It's Fitch, says he's tried to ring but can't get through and that he needs to talk to me urgently." Ant held the phone above his head at various angles trying to get a better reception. The signal strength indicator refused to budge above one bar. "We're lucky to live in Norfolk, Lyn, but sometimes it drives me mad."

Lyn gave the tiller a deft push to the right. "And you seriously think shaking your mobile like a rag doll will improve reception?"

Ant glared at his phone, then gave Lyn a look of resignation. "It's not like Fitch to be so persistent; you know how laid back he normally is. Let's head back to the Hall and give him a ring."

———————

"Your stupid car should know its own way to the cottage by now."

Ant smiled as the Morgan swept out of Stanton Parva and settled into what had become a familiar journey over the last five days. "Fitch was clear what the garage guy said. If the old fella did sell Jack Spinner a new SIM card this morning, that must mean he's back at what passes for home."

Lyn looked across to her companion. "But it could have been anyone. I bet that bloke serves dozens of people a day. It would be easy to confuse one man in his early thirties with another."

"Let me ask you a question: do you get the kids at your school mixed up?"

Lyn threw him a confused look. "Of course not, I make it my business to get to know each one of them."

He briefly raised a hand from the steering wheel to indicate mild irritation. "Then why don't you believe a bloke who's owned a garage for donkey's years, serving the same locals day after day, has a reasonable recollection of who he sold a SIM card to this morning?"

The remainder of the journey took place in comparative silence as minds raced in anticipation of, at last, speaking to Jack Spinner and finding out, once and for all, what actually happened ten years earlier and, more importantly, what Jack knew about Amber's death.

Ant eased off the accelerator well before he reached the

fallen tree trunk that disguised the entrance to the cottage. The only sound permeating an otherwise quiet landscape was that of the car's tyres crunching an assortment of dry leaves and twigs, which lay scattered over a narrow soil strip between the road and treeline. Indicating for Lyn to exit the Morgan as quietly as she could, Ant joined her as they made for the camouflaged hazel panel that hid the narrow trackway to the cottage.

"That doesn't look good, Ant. Somebody has moved it aside."

They both now stood in front of the half-opened disguise.

"And it can't have been Jack Spinner after spending years going to the trouble of hiding from the world and his mother."

Hesitantly, they moved forward, taking care not to stand on anything that might give their presence away. Within a minute the quaint sight of the little thatched cottage, framed by a backdrop of trees and a neatly tended vegetable patch presented itself.

"It all looks normal to me." Lyn remained close to Ant as she spoke.

"Something's not right. Look at the front door; it's open a few inches. Perhaps Jack has been and gone and didn't bother to lock up because he wasn't coming back... or—"

Lyn completed his sentence. "Or he's had an unwelcome visitor?"

Reaching the front door, Ant gently pressed a hand to the bleached paintwork. The door swung slowly backwards, its hinges creaking in protest. He gestured for Lyn to take a look around the back while he searched inside. Moving stealthily from room to room as if he were on active service,

Ant's eyes darted from one area to the next to make sure they missed nothing.

Failing to stop the stair tread from creaking no matter how he tried, he decided to minimise the time he spent on them and leapt up the remaining steps two at a time. Again, he moved from room to room with purpose and discipline. Ant soon realised the building was empty. He looked out of a rear bedroom window, its glass coated in a thick layer of dirt from years of neglect.

Moving one half of the threadbare cotton curtains aside, Ant looked down on a scattering of dishevelled outbuildings rapidly being reclaimed by nature. Suddenly his gaze was drawn to something moving, and he strained to see through the weather-stained window glass. He saw Lyn. She had come out of a large timber building. Now she stood motionless, seemingly staring back into the structure.

Ant scurried down the carpet-less stairs, and his foot slid on something as he crossed the stone floor of the tiny hallway.

So he was *here.*

Ant picked up a blister pack that appeared to have been ripped open. It had contained a SIM card.

Walking at pace to where Lyn was, adrenaline began to pump through his body as he neared his statue-like friend. "What's the matter?"

She didn't answer. Soon he understood why. Ant looked into the broken-down building. He saw the body of a man lying on a bed of detritus that had accumulated in the building over decades.

After taking a few minutes to diligently survey the tragic scene without disturbing anything, Ant turned to Lyn. "I know it's a shocking sight, but we have to get on. Lyn, I want you to phone Inspector Riley. Give him a heads-up. I'll ring Lister and get him over here."

Lyn's eyes flashed.

"I know, but we have no choice, Lyn."

"So you just happened to come across the body, did you?" Commander Lister's tone left no doubt that he considered Ant and Lyn's presence more than a coincidence. "I've been told about you two. Death seems to follow you around like a bad smell."

It took all of Ant's considerable willpower not to bite at Lister's provocation. "We could have just left the scene, Commander Lister. Had I decided to do that, you have my assurance that when Jack Spinner was eventually found, no one would have had the slightest idea that either Lyn or I had been anywhere near this place. Do we understand each other?"

Lister simply shrugged his shoulders and turned back to the body while barking orders to four constables to search the immediate area for anything unusual.

This left Lister and Ant in the decrepit outhouse. After a few minutes Lister looked behind him. "Why are you still here? Is there anything you wish to add to your earlier statement? If not, perhaps you will do the courtesy of collecting your friend and leaving me to my investigations."

Ant's blood was up. "Is that something you would like me to brief my father about?"

Lister held fire for a few seconds before composing himself and responding to Ant's challenge. "I promised your father to keep you involved. Instead, I find it is you who are continuing involving me in what is clearly a tragic dispute between two people who have been in hiding for ten years. Perhaps it all got too much. This is a classic murder-suicide. Jack Spinner murdered Amber Burton then, via some means I am yet to discover, took his own life. There's nothing more to it than that. Now, please leave before I order my men to remove you both."

Ant saw no point in arguing further, so turned on his heels as Lister bent down beside the body.

What's the point?

As he neared a still-motionless Lyn, he noticed she was looking past rather than at him. "Come on, Lyn. Did you get through to Peter Riley?"

She gave an almost imperceptible nod as Ant gently clasped her hand and led her back to the Morgan. As he opened the passenger door for her, Lyn caught Ant's eye. "He took something from beneath Jack's jacket."

The statement startled Ant. "He what?"

Lyn settled herself into the passenger seat. "As you walked back to me, Lister must have spotted something under Jack's coat. It was as if he were looking for something."

EVEN IN HIGH SUMMER, Cromer could be a chilly place if the wind streamed down from the north. As Ant and Lyn headed to the beach to meet Riley, he pulled up the zip on his summer jacket to offer at least some protection. He noted Lyn did not feel the need to do the same.

"You've got different blood from me, that's for sure." He waited for her to respond.

"Lyn, I said you must have... You're not listening, are

you?" He looked to his right; she seemed lost in her own world.

"Perhaps it was Jack after all? Ten years in hiding must have been tough on them both. What if he wanted his freedom, but Amber disagreed? Might he have decided the only way to escape their situation was to get rid of the problem?"

Blimey, where did that come from?

"I doubt it, Lyn. You don't give ten years of your life to suddenly change your mind. We need to look somewhere else for Amber's killer. We owe it to her, and her father.

"And Jack, Ant. Don't forget Jack."

Silence fell as Ant mulled over Lyn's words. Perhaps she was right; was he overthinking their whole approach?

Let's see what Riley says.

The harassed-looking man trying to control a lively springer spaniel stood out like a sore thumb.

"Look at this, makes you wonder who owns whom."

Lyn raised a smile as she watched Riley command his dog to behave, without success.

"Lucy, heel; come here, girl, or there's no treats for you tonight. Is that what you want?"

The two friends watched as the dog wound it's lead around Riley, literally tying him up in knots.

"Ten quid that Riley topples over."

"Evens at best, I reckon, Ant."

Thank heavens she's back.

A second later the lively animal caught sight of the two friends and started to bound over. Once her remaining lead ran out, the springer spaniel simply pulled Riley over, providing just enough slack in her lead to make it to Ant and Lyn. The dog's tail wagged manically as it tried to lick Lyn's knee.

"Ah, there you are. Not like you two to be late." Riley

spoke from a reclined position with outstretched arms as if it were the most natural position in the world from which to offer a greeting. "Come here, Lucy, you are a naughty girl, and Daddy will ground you if you don't behave."

Ant gave Lyn a bemused look.

"It's called anthropomorphism."

"What is?"

"When a person imposes human characteristics on an animal, it's called anthropomorphism."

Ant shook his head. "I have a shorter word I could use."

Managing to free himself from a tangle of material, Riley got to his feet and dusted the wet sand off his jacket and trousers. "A lively breed, springer spaniels. I used to have a golden retriever. Much better behaved but it had terrible wind trouble. Stank the house out, but she was a lovely old thing."

Ant wanted to speak, but the words wouldn't come as he watched Riley's eyes mist over.

"Never mind, at least this one keeps me fit."

Ant decided to move matters on rather than chance Riley having a complete breakdown. "So Lyn briefed you on Jack Spinner?"

Riley suddenly focused on his two companions. "Yes, and an odd do it is too."

Lyn nudged Ant.

Oh well, in for a penny, in for a pound.

"The thing is, Inspector Riley, we need your help."

Ant's request took Riley by surprise. His eyes widened, and he seemed to have lost all interest in trying to control Lucy.

I'm only asking for your help, not giving you a million quid.

"I see. Well, er, yes, of course. That's what we agreed to do, wasn't it, and, please, do call me Peter."

He'll want to invite us out for dinner next.

"The thing is, er, Peter, we need to know if Lister is still freezing you out of the investigation of Amber's death?"

Riley offered a weary smile. "Let's just put it this way; he's got me doing community policing talks to women's institutes, knitting circles, and church coffee mornings. Oh yes, and the local old people's homes, where even the staff have difficulty remembering what day it is."

Ant smiled. "Ah, yes. That tells me all I need to know, Peter."

"And archived information?" asked Lyn.

He shook his head. "He's cleared the lot. It's as if Amber never existed. It's all locked up in his... I mean, my office. Would you believe he's even managed to get the computer files locked, citing a hacking issue and that he's only following established force protocols. A load of codswallop if you ask me, but he's got everyone, except the goons he brought with him, terrified. He really is a piece of work."

Ant looked at Lyn, despair beginning to set in.

"But I did pick up one interesting titbit. My desk sergeant says there was talk of Lister being, how shall I put this, a little over-friendly towards certain young ladies when he was stationed here."

Ant looked at Lyn, who shrugged her shoulders. "Didn't you say Amber was acting oddly in the weeks leading up to her supposed boating accident?"

Lyn looked at Ant, then the detective. "Well, yes, but... I mean she didn't—"

"Didn't say anything to you," interjected Riley. "That's not unusual in these circumstances. Now, of course, there's no proof such a thing happened, but, as you know, my desk sergeant is not one for idle gossip."

Lyn's shock continued. "I suppose if Lister was bothering

her, she felt trapped. She could hardly speak to her father because he despised Jack Spinner. Perhaps she thought the only way to escape was to literally disappear and got Jack to go along with it?"

Ant stroked Riley's dog before getting up and clapping his hands together, causing Lyn and Riley to jump, and Lucy to start barking. "Then we need a plan. Peter, I think you should talk to Amber's father on the QT, and I'll chat to one of my intelligence contacts to see if the service has anything interesting on Lister. Okay, let's get to it."

Ant's sudden burst of decision-making set the air fizzing with activity as Riley suddenly exerted control over the springer spaniel.

"And I've got an idea—why don't I invite Kelly Jarvis out for a working lunch? That'll surprise her after all these years. Let's see what she remembers about threatening Amber."

"Fantastic idea, Lyn. Perhaps things aren't quite so dark as we thought a couple of hours ago."

Ant turned to Riley. "Thanks for meeting us, Peter. I can't tell you how useful it's been."

Oh no. He's starting to fill up again.

"It was my pleasure, Anthony. You know, after all this is over, I think we should all go out for dinner."

I knew it.

Two minutes later, Ant and Lyn were leaning against the Victorian cast-iron railing on Cromer Pier looking back at Riley kneeling down next to Lucy and allowing the animal to lick his face.

"Do you know, Ant, I think that man is genuinely lonely."

12

BURDEN OF RESPONSIBILITY

"You seem a bit brighter this morning, young lady," chirped Ant as he climbed out of his Morgan at Fitch's Automotive Services and greeted his best friend. "Perhaps the walk helped?"

"Walk? You mean all fifty steps from my place to here? Something tells me you've had too much caffeine this morning."

The friends smiled at each other as they looked around the untidy garage lot.

"Come out, come out, wherever you are."

A few seconds later, Fitch appeared from under a sorry-looking Volvo and wiped his hands with an already oily rag as he popped his head above a side wing of the old car. "What's he been drinking?"

Lyn's smile broadened. "There you are; that's two of us now. I'll have to have a word with your butler to ration you to two cups at breakfast."

Ant pulled a pained look, sharing it equally between his companions. "Very funny, I'm sure. As a matter of fact, I see it as my duty to bring sunshine into this hurting world each morning. When I look at you two, I know I've got my work cut out."

Fitch gave his hands a final rub with the filthy cotton material that served as an all-purpose cleaner and shook his head. "Come on, Lyn, let's get him into my office for a mug of my special brew to purge all that nasty caffeine from his brain cells, if there are any to be found."

Ant shuddered to a halt at the mention of the special brew. "You don't mean... that awful stuff?"

Fitch gave him a superior look. "I'll have you know I bought a job lot of it from a trusted source, and—"

"Fitch,   Doug   I-Can-Get-You-Anything-You-Want Smithers is about as trustful as a magpie in a silver shop. As for that special brew of yours, I bet the next mug who showed interest was told the stuff was excellent at cleaning brass doorknobs, descaling kettles, and getting rid of warts."

The mechanic ignored Ant's scepticism, lifted his head slightly, and sniffed the air. "Ah, just smell that, the sweet smell of perfection."

Ant glanced at an oil-covered percolator bubbling away wedged between some brake pads and several boxes of latex gloves. "All I can smell is brake fluid, and if you think I'm going to drink that stuff, you've another think coming."

A quiet cough, as if someone were clearing their throat, distracted both men.

"When you two idiots have finished playing games with each other, perhaps we might find somewhere to sit down in this tip and discuss what we came here for in the first place?"

Lyn's look of disapproval required obedience. "I believe you do own some chairs, Fitch? Oh yes, look, I can see four bits of wood touching the ground buried under all that rubbish."

Fitch looked at Ant, then Lyn, his confused expression clear for all to see. "Rubbish? I'll let you know I have every issue of *Popular Mechanics* since—"

"Don't say it, because it's not true, Fitch. That magazine has been going in one guise or another since 1902."

Fitch ignored Ant's fact check. "Since I started my apprenticeship."

Lyn went in for the kill. "Oh, so you have almost every edition, then?"

Fitch tilted his head to one side, refusing to bite on Lyn's sarcastic comment. Clearing away an armful of assorted vehicle parts and paperwork, three rickety chairs slowly began to appear from their concealment. "You're doing me a favour really. I try to catch up on my books on a Friday morning before the weekend rush begins."

Ant looked around the chaotic scene and had his doubts. "Anyway, mate, to business. Did you manage to ring the old bloke at the garage yesterday like I asked?"

Fitch lifted an index finger into the air as if he were about to reveal an earth-shattering piece of information. "I said I would, so I did. And what a conversation we had."

Ant glanced across at Lyn as she desperately tried to keep her balance on her wonky chair. "Go on, Fitch." He leant forward in anticipation.

Fidgeting with an exhaust bracket he'd just received to fit onto the Volvo, Fitch offered his guests an earnest look. "Do you know how hard it is to make a profit from a small petrol station and grocery store?" He didn't wait for a response. "No, and neither did I, but Albert gave me chapter and verse on how it was impossible to compete with the big chains of petrol stations. He reckons he can't buy stuff for the price the big boys are selling it for—"

Ant cut across his enraptured friend. "That's all very

interesting, but did he mention any odd stuff he noticed early yesterday?"

"Indeed, he did."

Ant's anticipation grew, and he could see Lyn leaning forward to hear more before she corrected her balance to stave off an awkward fall from her wobbly chair. "And...?"

"Well," Fitch continued enthusiastically, "Albert told me about a visit from—"

The garage phone rang. "It's the police. I recognise the number." Fitch snatched the desk phone from its cradle and announced himself. "I see, okay, about fifteen minutes. Thanks."

His two guests looked on expectantly.

"Got to go, I'm afraid. There's been a breakdown on the Northern Distributor Road, and the police want the car shifted, pronto, to head off a massive tailback."

Fitch leapt to his feet and headed out of the tiny, unkempt office. "Lock up, will you? You know where the spare keys are. Catch up later, yes?"

Ant looked stunned as he turned to a confused-looking Lyn. Taking a couple of seconds to digest what had just happened, Ant made a dash for the forecourt as Fitch fired up a huge vehicle recovery lorry.

"What about the old bloke?"

Fitch cupped a hand to his ear and Ant gestured for him to lower his window.

"I said, what about the old bloke?"

Fitch raised a thumb as he started to move off. "He mentioned a young couple turning up and giving him some patter about checking on listed buildings in the area. They had heard about a small cottage locally and could he point them in the right direction."

Ant attempted a follow-up question, but Fitch was, by

now, driving out of the open gates of the workshop forecourt.

Ant rushed back into Fitch's office to meet a still-startled Lyn.

"You hear that?"

"Yes, but not sure I understand the significance?"

Ant lifted a small paper calendar off the dust-covered wall above Fitch's disorganised desktop and retrieved a set of keys. "What if that supposed listed-buildings officer was Kelly Jarvis; the bloke, well, I'm not sure about him, but it's too much of a coincidence, don't you think?"

Lyn shook her head. "But what about Lister? I thought he was the one acting suspiciously?"

Ant looked at the keys and selected the smaller of the two. "I'm as confused as you, Lyn, but I have a gut feeling that stuff is about to happen, and we need to understand what's going on, so let's split our forces. Riley texted me this morning to say he couldn't get to Amber's father. Apparently, Lister is on his back so he can't leave the station. That being the case, I'll shoot around to Sidney Burton's place to see if he reacts when I push him about Lister's apparent behaviour ten years ago."

"And why don't I invite Kelly Jarvis out for lunch. She's bound to be intrigued why I've made contact after all these years, especially after the comment she made to you the other day."

Ant clapped his hands. "Done deal, let's get to it. Meet you at the Wherry Arms at seven?"

Lyn shook her head. "Will you stop doing that? It drives me nuts."

"What?"

"That hand-clapping thing, makes you look like a seal entertaining visitors at a zoo in exchange for smelly fish."

"WHERE IS SHE?" Sidney Burton's voice was tinged with menace as he gestured for Ant to take a seat in the small, shabby lounge of his cottage."

"Lyn has gone to Norwich, so I thought it a good idea to see how things are with you, Sidn... may I call you Sidney?"

The man nodded as he slumped side-on in an old armchair several feet from his guest. "Gone shopping, then, 'as she?"

Ant offered the faintest of smiles. "Something like that."

Sidney Burton did not reciprocate. "At least she can go shopping. Not like my Amber."

The room fell silent as Burton fixed his gaze on a sun-faded photo of Amber, which held pride of place on a chipped-tile mantelpiece.

Ant was content to let things settle for a minute or two.

At least he's not chucked me out.

Ant looked around the small room, which didn't seem to have been touched for years and pondered what Sidney Burton did with himself all day. He looked for signs of alcohol, but detected none. Next, he scanned the space for a TV or radio, again, a complete absence of technology.

What an existence.

Eventually, Burton barked out some words with a grizzled voice. "You've not come here to talk about the weather. What do you want?"

Ant took things slowly, keeping his voice low and calm. "As I said, Sidney, I wanted to check how you are." He smiled at the still-grouchy man.

Burton shifted his gaze from the photo of his daughter to glare at his house guest. "Don't play with me or I'll pitch you out on your ear with my bare hands. Understand?"

Mourning or not, he's got quite a temper.

"You're right, Sidney, and I apologise. I am interested in how you're doing, but I also need to ask about things that happened ten years ago, and I know you will find that hard." Ant expected, and duly received, a look of raw emotion from a man who looked many years older than his age. "I know. I do understand, believe me."

Ant detected an immediate softening of Burton's demeanour.

"Your brother?"

Ant was taken aback by Burton's words. He hadn't expected him to reference Greg, but then again, he figured it was a small village. "Well, er, yes. You see, Sidney, I understand the pain you feel, the not knowing and, yes, the guilt. I feel all those things too."

Burton got to his feet, wandered over to the fireplace, and picked up Amber's photo.

Ant instinctively pressed the home key on his mobile and flicked through his images until a familiar face gazed back at his. He held the photo towards Sidney Burton, who returned the gesture by wiping the dust from the old photo frame and turning it towards Ant.

"Both at peace, now, Sidney. Nothing that can hurt them anymore. But we can try to find out what happened. It took me years to get to the truth about my older brother's car accident, but in the end I got there. With Amber, there's still a lot to do, but believe me, Sidney, Lyn and I are getting close."

Ant watched Burton tense at the mention of Lyn.

Time to have this out.

"You know, Sidney, you've got Lyn wrong. Did you know we only identified your daughter because of a bracelet Lyn had bought Amber all those years ago? Imagine how Lyn felt when she realised what she was looking at on that beach." Ant stopped talking to give Burton a chance for his words to sink in. It took a while, but eventually, Burton reacted.

"It wouldn't have been so hard if we hadn't argued. I always told her I loved her, especially after her mother died. But that night... I don't know, something snapped, and I shouted at her. I don't know why."

Ant got up from his chair and walked the few feet to where Sidney Burton was standing, still clutching the faded photo of his daughter. "You were angry because you thought you were losing Amber to her boyfriend, Sidney. Every father goes through it, but it's no reason for blaming Lyn; she misses your daughter every bit as much as you do: in a different way, yes, but a deep sense of loss all the same."

Burton gave the image one last brush with his hand before returning the photo to the mantelpiece. "He was no good, you know. Always keeping her out to all hours. I knew he was a bad 'un, but Amber wouldn't listen. I told her the boy she dumped for him was a better bet, but she just kept saying he was a creep and suffocated her. You know, not letting her do anything or see anyone unless he was with her. I didn't notice anything, so I don't know what she was on about, but she wouldn't listen, and look what happened."

Ant stretched for the photo. "May I?"

Burton nodded.

"What do you see, Sidney?"

Burton shot Ant a stern glance.

"Not a trick question. Please, just tell me what you see in the photo?" Ant spoke quietly, gently.

Burton took back the photo and focused his whole attention on the image.

"My smiling little girl."

Ant put a comforting hand on Burton's shoulder. "But that's just the point, Sidney, smiling, happy, yes, but not a little girl. She was a grown woman. I'm sure her mother and you raised her to be a confident, responsible person. Someone who was able to make decisions for herself."

Ant detected Burton's eyes beginning to mist over.

"Amber's mother was the one that always said to be ambitious, to do her own thing and not be bossed around by anyone. She knew her own mind, I'll give her that."

Ant re-took the photo and placed it back in position. "So not someone who was afraid to confront difficult situations?"

Burton slowly shook his head as his gaze dropped to a threadbare carpet.

"But she was frightened about something those last few weeks before she first disappeared, wasn't she, Sidney?"

Burton slowly raised his eyes to give Ant an empty stare. Tears now flowed freely down his cheeks.

"You've carried the burden too long, Sidney. Now it's time to share it with someone. If you don't, it will kill you eventually, and it's already been ten years. Mark my words, I've seen it happen."

Sidney completely broke down and sank into Ant's shoulder as he sobbed uncontrollably. Ant placed one arm around Burton's back and held him close. With his free hand he stroked the man's unkempt hair. "It's okay, Sidney, let it out. It's been too long. Just let it out."

The two men stood for what seemed an age, Burton's shoulders heaving up and down as the tears continued to flow. Eventually, Burton's body began to lose some of its rigidity; the crying subsided into a series of heavy sighs. Ant loosened his grip and looked at Burton's flushed face, the man's eyes bloodshot with raw emotion.

"Sit yourself down, Sidney. Let's get you comfortable." Ant helped Burton back into his chair, then retreated back to the fireplace.

Time to let him settle.

He kept his attention focused on Burton as the man eventually composed himself and sat quietly for several minutes. Then he began to speak in a calm, quiet voice.

"He told me that Jack Spinner was no good and would get my Amber into trouble."

Ant deliberately refrained from asking who Burton was talking about. "And you believed him?"

Burton raised his eyes from the floor to look up at Ant. "He said he knew things about Jack Spinner that I wouldn't like. Who was I supposed to believe, Amber or him? I told her about him, but she just got more upset. She said he just wanted her to stop seeing Jack Spinner so he could control her. I couldn't make sense of any of it. It went on for weeks. He would keep coming around when Amber was out. He went on and on about Jack. Didn't have a good word for the man. Then I would repeat what he'd said to Amber, but she got more and more hysterical and accused me of trying to split them up, and if I didn't stop, they would do something that would ruin my life."

Ant listened closely to both Burton's words and any subtext he might inadvertently be sharing. "But why didn't you believe your daughter? After all, you were telling me only a few minutes ago that she'd been raised to be her own person and not blindly follow what someone else wanted to do."

Burton's eyes began to fill again. "But he..." His words faded into silence.

"It's okay, Sidney, let's call it a day; you look exhausted.

Why don't you have a nap in the chair and if you feel like it, we can talk again sometime?"

Burton surprised Ant by shaking his head.

"If I'd have listened to my own daughter instead of him, things might have ended differently. If I had been easier on that Jack fella, perhaps they wouldn't have planned to disappear, and maybe she would be alive now." His head dropped again as he picked at the already worn fabric of the chair arm.

Ant decided to tease the stranger's name from Burton. "Was Steven Foster really that jealous?"

Burton's head shot up. He gave Ant a confused look. "Steven Foster, why do you mention him?"

Ant pressed on. "He was the man who tried to break Amber and Jack up, wasn't he?"

Burton shook his head. "Certainly, I liked the boy and would have preferred it if Amber had stuck with him, but as I told you, my daughter thought him a control freak; no, I'm not talking about him."

Ant pressed on. "Then who are you talking about, Sidney?"

The man looked Ant square in the face.

"That policeman, the one that's come back."

13

LUNCH WITH THE ENEMY

L yn left her MINI in the underground car park of the Norwich Forum, then walked through the city's ancient outdoor market and onto Gentleman's Walk. Turning left onto the busy thoroughfare, she walked a further hundred yards and peeled right into one of several small shop-lined streets that followed the city's medieval street plan.

As she passed through the narrow doorway of the Weaver's Coffee Shop and Restaurant, Lyn could see that Kelly Jarvis was already seated.

"Wonderful to see you after all this time, Lyn. Please, do come and sit down. To save time I've already ordered the house lunchtime special; I hope you don't mind?"

Some things never change.

Lyn smiled politely. "Wonderful to see you too. The lunch special is fine. I'll get the drinks, shall I?"

Kelly gave Lyn a sort of sickly smile, the one she had always found disconcerting. "Thanks for offering but no need, I've done that too."

Lyn sat opposite Kelly and studied her subject. The

years had been kind to the woman, and her dress sense and makeup were as perfect as Lyn remembered.

She must spend hours to look like that.

"So what have you been up to all this time?" Lyn picked up her napkin, shook it loose, and placed the brilliant-white cotton cloth across her lap, deliberately avoiding eye contact with Kelly.

Her lunch mate reprised that smile. "Where to start; well, after university to study architecture, I got sidelined into building conservation and ended sort of combining the two by joining the listed-building planning team. Now, how about you? You're a classroom assistant, aren't you? Must be so rewarding being with all those little ones every day. I'm not sure I'd have the patience."

Don't bite, that's what she wants.

"After my A levels, I took a year out to travel around Australia and New Zealand."

"Tie me kangaroo down, sport."

"What? Oh, you mean the record. Love the accent, Kelly."

She's bonkers.

"Anyway, after that I got a first at Cambridge and went into teaching." Lyn felt uneasy about bragging but figured Kelly needed calling out. "I did a couple of years in a tough inner-city school in London, then applied for the headship in Stanton Parva. That's all, really."

She detected Kelly's irritated body language and pondered how she might react. If Lyn's memory served her correctly, her lunch companion would come out fighting.

"I hated school. Then again you must have loved it. I seem to remember you always were the teacher's pet. How's that posh boy you used to hang about with getting on, by the way?"

Just then the food arrived, swiftly followed by two soft drinks. It gave Lyn just enough time to compose her response.

"You're right, Kelly, I did enjoy school. Not sure I agree about the teacher's pet bit given how often I ended up in detention, more than once because you set me up if my memory serves me right? As for Anthony Stanton, I'd have thought you could answer that yourself since you only saw him on Monday morning?"

It didn't surprise Lyn that Kelly didn't flinch at being caught out.

"I hope you like Cromer crab. After all, you live so close to where they land it."

"Perfect, Kelly, and so clever of you to remember my favourite drink is Pepsi-Cola."

"It's Coca-Cola, not Pepsi, Lyn."

"Really? Oh well, they all taste the same, don't they?"

Lyn smiled inwardly at Kelly's look in failing to provoke a reaction.

Yes! Now stop being silly, Lynda.

"Have you anything exciting on for the weekend, Kelly?"

Her lunch companion shrugged her shoulders as she played with her food and did a poor job at trying to conceal glancing at her mobile every time the screen lit up. "Not really, Stevie wants to go fishing off Southwold Pier. I'd prefer to visit Lavenham. Trouble is he's a bit of a philistine when it comes to history."

"Well, they're both a bit of a run from here, but I'm with you. I love Suffolk. The countryside seems so much softer than the Broads and Lavenham is a beautiful place. It makes you wonder how it managed to survive unaltered."

It was as if Lyn had lit a match; Kelly's demeanour instantly changed as she waxed lyrical about the rise and fall of the Suffolk village. "It's simple, really: economics. Lavenham made its fortune in the fourteenth and fifteenth centuries from the wool trade. Did you know by 1450 it was amongst the top twenty most wealthy settlements in England?"

Did you know it was Pepsi-Cola until 1961?

"That's interesting, Kelly, tell me—"

"But as cheap imports of wool started to flood into the country it went into a steep decline and sort of got left behind. Luckily for us, because the town was relatively isolated, the bulldozers didn't move in during the nineteen sixties like they did in so many other areas, which is why we can enjoy one of the most intact medieval towns in the country. Fascinating, isn't it?"

Oh yes, fascinating.

"I can see you are passionate about your subject, Kelly. Talking about passion, who's this Stevie chap? Come, spill the beans. Is he a hunk?"

Lyn picked up immediately that Kelly's passionate side had slipped away to be replaced by her more familiar persona.

"Stevie? Oh, you would know him better by his full name. Steven... Steven Foster."

Lyn felt herself tensing and fought hard not to show any outward reaction to her lunch partner. She knew Kelly would expect her to be shocked. To divert attention, Lyn manipulated her fork with precision to extract white meat from her crab and place it delicately into her mouth. She watched Kelly as the woman waited for a reaction. Lyn made her wait by taking a sip of her soft drink and patting away any food around her lips with her napkin. Now she was ready to strike back. "Would that be the same Steven Foster that went out with Amber Burton? Has he grown up any, because I remember him as a bit on the jealous side?"

She watched as the sickly smile evaporated from Kelly's cheeks.

"If you must know, he's a sweetie. A typical bloke when it comes to boys' toys and hobbies, but he's so attentive and never looks at another girl."

And pigs can fly.

Lyn took another sip from her drink, expertly moving three ice cubes out of the way with her paper straw. "That's good to hear, Kelly. You hear so much about infidelity these days. Makes you wonder why anyone bothers." Lyn knew she had shot herself in the foot as soon as the words came out of her mouth.

"Is that why you never married, Lyn? Are you afraid any man you let near will let you down? How are things between Anthony Stanton and you, anyway?"

Lyn knew she had to come out fighting. "Not at all, I've been more focused on my career, that's all. As for Ant, I'm not sure what you mean. We grew up together. I went travelling; he went into the army and now he's back. No mystery there, Kelly."

And that's all you're getting, madam.

Their game was interrupted by a waitress enquiring whether the food was okay. Both women smiled and nodded, allowing the server to melt quickly into the background of the busy restaurant. Silence descended as Lyn and Kelly tucked into their food. However, it wasn't long before the battle recommenced.

"I wasn't suggesting any mystery, Lyn. Just saying, people change and perhaps you two are not as close anymore."

What I'd give to throw this crab at you.

"Well, you'll have to be the judge of that. After all, you

saw him on Monday. Did he appear any different to you? Ant tells me you were the same old Kelly. Then again, wanting attention doesn't hurt anyone, does it?"

Kelly did that smile thing again. "He's a lot more handsome than I remember, that's for sure. But I'm not interested; I've got my Stevie."

Lyn returned her lunch partner's sickly smile. "Ah, yes, Steven Foster. How long have you been together?"

Kelly stirred the remains of her soft drink with a straw. "About ten years now, off and on."

Lyn's eyes narrowed. "Heck, that's a long time to be engaged, or whatever phrase people use these days. That means you hooked up at the same time Amber went missing?"

Kelly stopped toying with the paper straw. "What are you suggesting, Lyn?"

Getting somewhere at last.

"Suggesting, what do you mean? All I meant was Amber disappeared ten years ago, and you began going out with Steven Foster around that time. That's not a suggestion, Kelly, from what you've just said, it's a fact. Anyway, you always did have a soft spot for him. Must have irked you that he picked Amber instead?"

Just then the waitress reappeared to enquire if the two women would like a sweet. Neither answered, a wave of the head had to suffice. The server turned on her heel and left the combatants to their verbal duel.

Lyn's probing was having an effect. "I have no idea what you mean. Amber was my best friend; everyone knew that. It's just that we... when we thought Amber had died, Stevie and I spent time with each other; sort of grieving together I suppose, and we didn't get together for ages after, but then something happened, I don't know. Who knows what attracts one person to another? Well, as I said, we've been together on and off ever since. This time it's been two years."

Very convincing, girl.

"I know I wasn't as close as you were to Amber, Kelly. Even so, she told me Steven could be hard work, you know, always wanting to call the shots and checking who she was seeing, what she was doing, that sort of thing. Is he like that with you?"

Lyn immediately saw she'd touched a raw nerve.

"I don't know what you mean; don't be stupid. I wouldn't put up with that. Anyway, controlling is not the same as watching out for you. I'd say that's sweet."

Leopards and spots, I think.

"Anyway, do you want a coffee, Lyn?"

She smiled. "Yes, if you have the time. Why not?"

Lyn sat back in her chair and gave Kelly an intense look. "You know, not once since we sat down today have you mentioned Amber; how awful her being found dead is and if there is any link between the things that happened ten years ago and now. As you said, you were her best friend."

Lyn's question sent Kelly reeling. Gone was her composure, in an instant she broke down and made so much noise that diners at the nearby tables asked Lyn if everything was all right.

Now, that's what I call acting.

"Come on, Kelly. I'm sorry if I've upset you, but we've known one another long enough to speak plainly when we have to. Here, take this napkin." Lyn picked up a clean cloth form one of the other two place settings on the square table and offered it to her still-sobbing companion.

"It's just that... Oh, I don't know, I guess I've buried my feelings for so long that I didn't want to admit Amber is finally dead." She dabbed her eyes and placed the napkin onto the table.

Mascara still intact, then.

"I know, Kelly, it's been a tough time for all of us who knew Amber. Why don't we change the subject? Tell me a bit more about your work; it sounds fascinating."

Kelly picked up the napkin again, gave her eyes a final dab, scrunched up the cotton square, and dropped it back onto the table. "What is it you want to know?" she said in a quiet voice.

"Let me think. Yes, I know. Tell me about your clients or whatever you call them. You know, someone submits an application for listed-building planning consent, and your department ends up telling them they can't do... whatever? You must get into some interesting conversations."

Kelly looked past Lyn to smile at a waitress, who had brought the coffees, before turning her attention back to her lunch companion. "Well, it's true that people often want to make alterations to listed buildings that we have to say no to. For instance, one chap lived in a Tudor timber-framed house, you know, painted black and white with a thatched roof, a real chocolate-box look to it. Anyway, he wanted to put double glazing in, plastic window frames, the lot. We said it wouldn't be in keeping with the heritage of the building and he went nuts. The man appealed every decision we made, but we stuck by our guns. It put his building project back by eighteen months and he wasn't happy with us."

Lyn sipped from her coffee as Kelly waxed lyrical about her job. "Well, I can see the dilemmas you face, I guess almost every day. Common sense tells me it's more fruitful to work with, rather than kick against, the rules."

"You're so right, Lyn, but I suppose people get so

wrapped up in creating something they may have had in their head for years. But rules are rules."

"And thank heavens for them, Kelly. Does that go for Ant as well? I hear he wasn't too pleased about what was said to him about his stables project."

Kelly fell quiet for a few seconds. "You know, Lyn, I really can't talk about an individual case. All I can say is that we have some more talking to do."

Well done for heading that one off.

"Oh, I knew there was something else I wanted to ask you about your fascinating job. Does it involve a lot of travelling about, you know, a barn conversion at one end of the county, then rush to a Georgian coaching inn restoration at the opposite end? You must put a lot of miles in?"

Kelly looked into her coffee cup to see if there was more to be had and spoke without raising her head. "A fair bit, but it's mostly within forty miles of Norwich, so not too bad."

Lyn drank the last of her coffee and made to gather her jacket. "Oh well, that's sounds manageable, then. So no long trip out Sandringham way?"

Kelly gave Lyn a curious look. "No, not been out that way for months. Why do you ask?"

Lyn stood up and slipped her jacket on. "Oh, no reason. Come on, I'd better not keep you from work any longer or I'll be getting you into trouble."

After settling the bill, the two women stood outside on the cobbled street as Lyn began to say her goodbyes. "Well, at least we were able to share a few memories about Amber, and that was good, wasn't it? But what a tragic couple they were."

Kelly adopted her confused look again. "What do you mean?"

Lyn closed the space between them and spoke softly. "Well, first Amber, then Jack Spinner."

Her companion's face drained of colour. "Jack, what about Jack?"

Lyn feigned a look of horror. "Oh, I shouldn't have told you that. The police swore me to secrecy until they announce it publicly."

"Announce what?"

"That Jack Spinner was found dead yesterday. I know that the last time you saw Amber you threatened her, and, of course, your Stevie was a jealous one when he went out with Amber, but I'm sure the police won't try to say two and two make five."

Instead of looking panic stricken, Kelly was suddenly quite composed.

"You know, Lyn, there are those people who always think the worst of others. I try to see the best in people. Besides, I've always found the police to be perfectly amenable, but shh, don't tell anyone I said that, will you, at least not until Commander Lister makes an arrest."

14

AN ARRESTING TIME

F riday evening at Stanton Hall was, as usual, a hive of activity as the staff made sure everything was neat and tidy before leaving, so that the weekend skeleton staff would be able to manage anything the family needed.

"Ah, Jo, I thought I'd find you here." Ant closed the heavy oak door to the great hall behind him then stepped forward to welcome the planning officer.

"Lord Stanton, it was so generous of you to invite me to the Hall; I can't believe my luck. There are so many fascinating things to see here. I wish I could have been a fly on the wall to hear all the interesting conversations that have taken place in this room down the centuries."

"Believe me, Jo, if this place could talk, some of my family would have been for the high jump as they decided which side to back in various conflicts like the English Civil War. Luckily for us, Oliver Cromwell didn't think the place was worth blowing up when the family supported Charles I, but he did throw us out, and eventually we had to buy the estate back, so I suppose you could say we paid the price for being royalists."

Ant's potted history of his family's loyalty to the Crown seemed to intrigue Jo. "That must have been a brave thing to do."

He smiled. "Not really, look at the portraits around you. Most of my ancestors were very keen on the latest fashions. Think of the two options available during the Civil War. To be dressed like a tin can as part of the Roundheads' New Model Army, or wear fancy silk britches and jackets and a big feather in your even bigger hat."

She laughed. "Well, when you put it like that."

Ant closed in on a section of oak panelling that Jo had been paying close attention to when he came in. "What is it you found so fascinating about this?"

Jo turned back to the panelling and pointed to a small mark on the dark oak framing. "Do you see that daisy wheel pattern, just in the corner there? See, a little circle with what looks like six daisy leaves inside it?"

Ant leant forward. "Yes, but what does it signify?"

"Well, I guess the best way to describe the scratching is to give it its official name. They're called apotropaic marks. It's a Greek word for averting evil, and they date back to times when belief in witchcraft and the supernatural was widespread. So scratch one or more of these in each room, it means your house is protected from evil and bars entrance to anything that could harm you."

As Ant ran the tip of his finger over the mark, he heard the distinctive sound of the door to the great hall opening. Turning around he saw the butler, David, standing next to an immaculately dressed young woman.

"Miss Jemma Cole, sir."

"Hello, and welcome to Stanton Hall, Jemma. Jo and I have just been inspecting an apotropaic mark."

Jemma raised an eyebrow. "You mean a witch mark?"

Ant smiled. "I see you know your history. There's no catching you out, is there? Come and meet Jo Wayland. She's an expert in this stuff and works for the listed-building unit down at the planning office."

He watched as the two women gave each other the once-over and thought Jemma looked the more uncomfortable, presumably because she thought she would have his undivided attention. Meanwhile, Jo merely seemed intrigued at the presence of such a well-turned-out woman, who looked as though she was dressed for a night on the town.

"Here's what I think we should do. Jo is here to discover all she can about some of the Hall's more eccentric attributes, so I think we should leave her to get on with that. Jemma, I promised you the grand tour so why don't we make a start?"

He detected that Jo was quite happy to be left to continue her research, while Jemma still looked a little perplexed. "Come on, let's get going. There's nearly six hundred years of roof leaks and peeling Chinese wallpaper to show you."

Jemma took one last lingering look around the great hall before catching up with Ant, who was already halfway through the door.

"I don't see much evidence of damp, Anthony Stanton?"

"You just wait until we get to the attic rooms, then you'll see what it really takes to keep a place like this going."

"WHAT ON EARTH is the matter with you? You look like you've seen a ghost." Fitch closed the door of Lyn's MINI Clubman and guided her into his untidy office. "This isn't like you, come and sit down. I'll make you a mug of my special brew."

Lyn forced a smile and waved a hand to indicate she wasn't in the mood for one of his eccentric concoctions. "I've just had one of the most unpleasant few hours of my life, and that's saying something after the week we've all had."

Fitch flicked the electric kettle on and wiped the tea-stained interior of a mug with his forefinger. Peering into the empty container and satisfied it was fit for purpose, he placed it on the uneven surface of an old timber shelf and tossed a teabag into it.

"As you say, it's been a tough week, so what is it that was so unpleasant?"

She brushed her hands against her pencil skirt as if trying to wipe away some sort of contamination. "Not a what, it's a who. Do you remember Kelly Jarvis?"

Fitch frowned and shook his head.

"She was Amber's best friend, or at least that's what she used to tell everybody. I'm not so sure myself. Anyway, she works for the planning department and had a run-in with Ant at the beginning of the week. He reckons she spent more time flirting with him than doing her job. It seems she also made quite a point of asking him to remember her to me. Now, I haven't seen Kelly in ten years, but I still remembered how unpleasant she could be. Still, I suggested to Ant that I should meet her to see what she was about."

A distinct click told Fitch that the water had boiled. He turned, picked up the kettle, and poured the boiling liquid into the less-than-pristine mug. "And spending just an hour with that woman has done this to you? What on earth happened?"

Lyn's eyes began to fill with tears "It's not so much what she said, it's how she said it. We've never liked one another, and she does have a way of getting to me. Don't get me wrong, I gave as good as I got over lunch, and we spent most of the time playing verbal games with one another. Nevertheless, I came away with the distinct feeling she'd got the better of me."

Fitch gestured to his mug. "Are you sure you don't want one of my special brews?"

"I'm not being funny, Fitch. But I don't think even one of your concoctions would take the edge of how I'm feeling at the moment."

Fitch played with his mug. "Come to think of it, I do remember her. Wasn't she the one that caused all that trouble between you and Amber?"

Lyn's tears began to flow. "I guess it was as much my fault as hers. I knew she was provoking me, but she reeled me in like a fish on the end of the line."

Fitch placed his drink back on the wobbly shelf, rummaged about in an open drawer, and retrieved a cellophane-covered pack of tissues. "Here, I think you need these."

Lyn glanced at the tissues and failed to hide her surprise at their immaculate condition. "Wonders will never cease. Now, be honest, how long have they been in that drawer?"

He looked back at the ancient storage cupboard. "Beggars can't be choosers, Ms Blackthorn. Anyway, they're wrapped in plastic, so grab hold of one and blow your nose; think of what your school students will think if they saw you like this."

Lyn did as she was instructed and tried to disguise the sound of her clearing her nostrils as best she could. "Not a lot. You do have a way with words, don't you, Fitch."

He smiled, turned to his hot drink, and began to sip from the discoloured earthenware.

"So tell me what happened between Kelly and you all those years ago. If I remember correctly, you ended up in the police station?"

Lyn dabbed her nose for the final time before throwing the squashed-up tissue into a nearby waste bin which took the form of an empty twenty-five-gallon tin of engine cleaning fluid cut in half.

"Thanks for remembering the good bits, Fitch. As it happens, she accused me of stealing a gold bracelet she said she'd bought for Amber. I don't recall ever seeing such a thing until the police were called and I had to empty my pockets. And guess what, the gold bracelet was found in my jacket. Amber was furious with me and became hysterical. Her father called me words I'd never heard before. But do you know the thing I remember most? That sickly smile that Kelly Jarvis excelled at. It was that which I saw again today over lunch."

Fitch took another gulp from his mug, wiped his mouth with the back of an oily hand, and placed the container into a sink, which Lyn had, for years, refused to go near.

"Yes, you're right, I remember now. I suppose it was lucky for you Fred got to the bottom of it, and who says it doesn't pay to have friends in the police?"

Lyn let out a sigh. "It wasn't so much that he got to the bottom of it but proved I hadn't put the bracelet in my jacket. I'd inadvertently left it in the chip shop at lunchtime. It wasn't until I got to Amber's a couple of hours later that I realised what I'd done."

"So how did you get it back?"

Lyn gave Fitch a resigned look. "Kelly said the woman from the chip shop gave it to her knowing we knew one another. But I couldn't prove Kelly had put the bracelet in my pocket. The police couldn't pin it on me because the jacket had been out of my possession for hours. In the end they let the matter drop, although they did hang on to the bracelet since Kelly couldn't provide a receipt for it."

Fitch played with a pen as he sat on the edge of his disorganised desk. "I can see why there's no love lost between you two, so what happened after that little incident?"

"I got the impression Amber still wasn't convinced about me, so I bought her a charm bracelet, and—"

"And that was the bracelet you found on Amber's wrist last Saturday morning?"

Lyn nodded. "You can see what effect all of this has had on me. To cap it all, Jack Spinner is also dead, and neither Ant nor I have the first clue about what's going on."

Fitch shuffled off his desk, threw a pile of papers on the floor allowing him access to an old wooden chair, and sat down facing Lyn. "Chin up. You know Ant and you always sort it out in the end. So, come on, what's next?"

Lyn took another tissue from its cellophane wrapper and cleared her nose. "Time, I think, for a nice long bath to soak away any thoughts of Kelly Jarvis. Then I've got the delightful treat to look forward to, spending my evening in the Wherry Arms with you and the other musketeer."

"So that's Stanton Hall in all its glory, Jemma. Eighty-nine rooms, the odd family ghost or two, and more buckets to catch rainwater than you can shake a stick at."

Jemma's eyes darted from one precious artefact to the next as Ant walked her down the grand staircase and into the morning room. On the large oval table in the centre of the sumptuous room stood a silver cake stand accompanied by two small silver trays of petite sandwiches minus their crusts, and an ornate tea pot with an elegant spout. Fine bone china plates and all the other paraphernalia to make ready for a traditional English afternoon tea completed the ensemble.

"Wow, I didn't expect this."

"Well, I did promise you the full works. The only bit I can't deliver is the presence of my father, the Earl. He's busy with one of his charities and sends his apologies."

"Of course, yes, I absolutely understand."

"Ah, David. Wonderful timing."

The butler showed Jo through the already open door. "Do join us, Jo. David and his staff have done us proud."

The butler offered the slightest of nods in acknowledgement of the compliment, stepped back and gently closed the door.

Ant hoped the passage of a couple of hours with each woman having been engrossed in their separate interests might make for more convivial company than earlier. He was pleasantly surprised.

"It's such a marvellous place, Jo. You're so lucky that Ant has allowed you free access to do your, oh, what was that word? Never mind, you know what I mean, the witch thing."

"Yes, I absolutely know how fortunate I am; I can't thank Ant's family enough. And to cap it all, afternoon tea."

Thank heavens for that.

The next twenty minutes were spent in pleasant conversation as they each tucked into a sumptuous variety of dainty cakes and wafer-thin sandwiches.

"Well, this has got to be better than chasing stories for your newspaper about the latest dog that's gone missing. Not sure about you, though, Jo. I think your working day must be so interesting even if some of the people you meet in your professional capacity are a bit angry with you at times."

The two women looked at one another and exchanged smiles. "How do you know about all those shaggy-dog stories I have to write, Anthony?"

"Just an educated guess, Jemma. After all, and I don't mean to sound discourteous, but the local free newspaper is hardly the same as the *London Times*, now, is it?"

Jemma laughed as she tucked into another mini chocolate éclair. "I can't argue with that."

Jo joined the banter. "So you chase stories about dogs all week, Jemma, while I look for scratches in plasterwork and cobweb-covered attics. And I hate spiders."

Several minutes passed as the threesome ate their fill and drained the last of the tea.

"At least you're not rushing around the county, Jo, or are you? I suppose you have a large area to cover?"

Jo smiled at Ant. "It's not too bad. Site visits are a normal part of the job, but depending on what's being discussed, not all of us go out to every call."

"Remind me, again, how many of you are in the department?"

Jo hesitated as she mentally totalled up the size of her department. "Eight altogether. Although Kelly and I spend most of our time in the office."

Ant's curiosity got the better of him. "So no trips out to the King's Lynn area recently?"

Jo thought for a moment. "Let me think. Well, certainly not me, but now you mention it, Kelly's been out there a couple of times over the last few days, lucky thing with all this lovely weather."

"It's easy to tell when it's your round, Ant—you're always late."

"And good evening to you, Fitch. There's nothing like a warm welcome, is there?"

Ant grinned as he walked up to the small round table occupied by his two best friends and sat down on a sturdy stool. He caught the bar manager's eye and shouted the drinks order loud enough to be heard above the general hubbub of the busy pub. "There, are you satisfied now?"

"I'll be satisfied when I take a first sip of my pint."

Lyn was more gracious. "That's very kind of you, Ant. I know how hard that must have been."

All three broke into laughter at the running gag of Ant's deep pockets and short arms.

"At last." Fitch sighed as Jed placed a battered metal tray on the table, causing two of the three drinks to shed a minute quantity of their contents. "Jed, it's good beer you're spilling, mate. That's sacrilege, that is."

The bar manager shrugged, turned a hundred eighty degrees and sauntered back to the bar.

Several minutes of quiet reflection followed as Fitch savoured his pint of lager, Ant devoured his Fen Bodger pale ale, and Lynn delighted in sipping her gin and tonic.

"Come on, Lyn. Tell me about your afternoon with the wonderful Kelly, and I'll give you all the latest gossip from the listed-buildings planning department."

He immediately knew he'd put his foot in it as he watched Lyn and Fitch freeze. "Have I said something wrong?"

Fitch shot Lyn a knowing look.

"Come on, what's up?"

Ant could see Lyn looked uncomfortable. It took quite

an effort to get her to open up as she relayed the outcome of a meeting with Kelly.

"That name again. First of all, she spends most of her time over at the Hall batting her eyelashes at me. Then you reckon she might have some kind of connection to our dear Commander Lister, let alone Amber's ex. Then to cap it all, one of her work colleagues told me a little earlier that she spent a number of days in the King's Lynn area this week."

Lyn's eyes flashed. "King's Lynn?"

Ant looked confused. "Yes, that's what Jo said."

"But that means she lied to me when I asked her the very same thing. She told me she hadn't been out of the office since seeing you up at the Hall."

The bar fell suddenly silent as all eyes focused on the two narrow entrance doors to the pub. A plain-clothed detective flanked with two heavyset, uniformed constables strode confidently into the small space and approached Ant's table.

What's Lister up to?

"Ms Lynda Blackthorn. Lord Anthony Stanton. I am arresting you on suspicion of murdering Amber Burton and Jack Spinner."

15

FORTITUDE

Having each spent an uncomfortable night in Stanton Parva police station, Ant and Lyn were pleased to be back at Stanton Hall even if they were surrounded by the family's legal team.

"You say he just stumped up to you in the pub last night?" Ant's father gave his son a perplexed look as he tried to take in the events of the last twelve hours. "It seems to me that Commander Lister has some explaining to do, and mark my words, explain to me he will."

The family butler, David, made himself busy refilling tea cups and making sure there was plenty of toast and Danish pastries to keep all present satisfied.

Lyn turned to Ant. "What did Lister want to know?"

Extending a hand to select one of the pastries, he savoured the sweet smell of the treat before turning his attention back to his friend. "It wasn't so much what he wanted to know as what he insisted on telling me. In short, I seem to have been responsible for every murder in Norfolk over the last twelve months. He also said you told him I'd forced you to help kill Amber Burton and Jack Spinner."

Lyn smiled as she lifted a delicate cup up to her lips. Blowing across the top of the fine china to cool its contents, she took the smallest of sips. "Funnily enough he said exactly the same to me except, of course, all roles were reversed."

Ant turned to ask Sir Geoffrey Bamber, Queen's Counsel, what he thought Commander Lister was playing at.

Six feet two, soberly dressed, and of a serious demeanour, Sir Geoffrey peered at Ant over his half-rimmed glasses. "I don't think either of you have anything at all to be concerned about. In my experience, Commander Lister's behaviour is nothing more than a fishing expedition, and fishing without a rod at that. From what you've told me about the events of the last week and, frankly, the peculiar reappearance of Commander Lister to take control of the investigation, I am of the opinion that for reasons yet unknown, his intention was to keep both of you off the streets, so to speak, in order for him to complete his, as of yet unknown, endeavour."

Why use one word when you can use twenty?

Ant took Lyn's cup and walked over to a mahogany buffet, leaving her to pick up the conversation with the redoubtable Queen's Counsel.

"Well, if that were his intention, it didn't work too well, did it?"

Sir Geoffrey gave a rare smile. "I hesitate to suggest that my own humble intervention had anything to do with your release; however, it was clear he intended to keep both of you in detention for as long as possible. Unfortunately for the good commander, his understanding or, at the very least, interpretation, concerning the law of custody was, shall we say, not commensurate with his high rank."

A roar of laughter interrupted the sedate atmosphere of

the spacious office. "My dear Geoffrey, I am so glad I do not pay you by the spoken word, for I should now be bankrupt."

Sir Geoffrey broke into a rare second smile. "But you do pay for my time. Therefore, the number of words I speak in any given consultation has a direct impact on the size of your bill."

"He's got you there, Dad."

"You are correct, son. There goes another two hundred and fifty pounds. Anyway, would anyone like another Danish?"

The Earl of Stanton's sanguine response caused a ripple of laughter to reverberate around the oak-panelled surfaces of the ancient room.

Sir Geoffrey's smile didn't take long to merge back into his more usual sober demeanour. "Now, Anthony. While we have had much merriment over the last short while, we should not forget the, if I may say so, onerous bail conditions, which have been set for both Miss Blackthorn and you. Please, do remember that you must not leave Stanton Hall until you appear before the magistrate. Do I make myself clear?"

Ant's smile also slipped, to be replaced by irritation. "So Lister accomplishes what he set out to do. Whether Lyn and I are stuck in a prison cell or held captive at the Hall, the result is the same."

Lyn let out an almost imperceptible cough by way of calling attention to herself. "Of course, there is a difference between being told not to leave the Hall and, in fact, being seen to leave the premises."

Ant detected a sparkle in his best friend's eyes and saw no need to either agree or contradict her point.

"That is not for me to comment upon," said Sir Geoffrey in his trademark gravelly voice. "All I can say is that you have both signed to say you will obey the bail conditions. As your legal representative, I am certain you will now reassure me that that is indeed what you intend to do."

Now it was the father's turn to cough. "A two-word response will suffice, son. I see that Sir Geoffrey's billing period is about to leap into a fourth hour." He smiled and winked at the QC.

"Of course," responded Ant, tapping the side of his nose with a forefinger.

Sir Geoffrey placed his fine china cup and saucer onto a low mahogany table in front of him, straightened himself up as far as his rotund figure would allow, and ran the palm of his right hand down his waistcoat to dislodge any remnants of Danish pastry which dared to have lodged there. "Then that is all we need say on the matter. Now, my colleagues and I wish you good morning, for we have the eleven o'clock London train to catch." The QC turned to Lyn, then the Earl of Stanton, and finally Ant, giving a polite nod to each. Ant's father gave a discreet signal to the butler, who quietly acknowledged the instruction, opened the ornately panelled door and escorted the visitors to the waiting car.

"He's as dry as salt, isn't he?"

"You may say that, son, but he's the best in the business and most prosecuting counsel fear him. In that regard, you two should take comfort in knowing that Lister stands little chance of getting away with whatever he's up to. Now, I am commanded by your mother to join her in the conservatory. It seems a new orchid has flowered, and I must be seen to admire it. Behave, you two, do you understand?"

Both beamed at the old gentleman.

"I mean it. Don't give Lister any opportunity to put you back in the cells, because it will take me six hours to get Sir Geoffrey here to work his magic a second time."

This time a nod sufficed, allowing the Ant's father to leave the room with at least some hope that the two miscreants might behave themselves.

Ant appeared shell shocked as he took in the events of the last twelve hours. Looking across to Lyn, he could see she felt the same. "You know what, it's nice to have some peace and quiet now that lot have gone, plus we haven't got Lister breathing down our necks, at least for the time being."

Lyn wandered over to check on tea supplies. "Want some?"

"Why not, there's not much more we can do for the time being. Any Danish pastries left?"

Lyn flashed Ant a critical look as she pointed to a silver dish piled high with the sweet treats. "One or two?"

He gave her one of his cheeky-boy grins. "Two, please."

The couple enjoyed ten minutes' peace before their solitude was interrupted. A gentle creaking noise from behind alerted them to a new arrival in the spacious room.

"Oh, sorry. I didn't know anyone was in here."

Realising who it was, Ant stood and stretched out a welcoming hand. "Hello Jo, nice to see you again. On the hunt for more of those witches' marks?"

"Ah, you mean apotropaic marks," said Lyn.

Ant shook his head. "You as well? Is it only me that has never heard that word before?"

The two women laughed.

"Actually, I'd never heard of it myself until I started to work with the planning department."

"And what's your excuse? Don't tell me, you're a head teacher."

Lyn gave a broad smile. "What can I say?"

He watched as the two women enjoyed his embarrassment and decided to move the conversation on. "Actually, it's quite opportune that you've popped in. Lyn and I have been talking about one of her old friends. She's also known to you."

"I'm intrigued."

"Good, why don't you sit down and join us; tea?"

She nodded, and thirty seconds later, Ant delivered her drink. "Sorry if it's a little on the cool side; it's been in the pot for quite a while."

Jo looked down at her drink. "It'll be fine, I'm sure. Now, tell me, who is this mystery person?"

Lyn took over the conversation. "Kelly Jarvis. We both grew up around here. Ant has told me that you both work in the same department. We just wondered if you could tell us anything about her, you know, easy to work with, a bit of a pain, that sort of thing?"

Jo took a sip of her tea. "Well, I suppose she's okay to get along with most of the time. Of course, we all have our off days, don't we?"

Lyn frowned. "You can say that again. When she has an off day, does it tend to be caused by anything in particular?"

"That's an odd question. I'm not sure what you mean?"

Ant jumped in. "That's okay, Jo. It's not meant as a trick question. However, we are interested in how Kelly Jarvis behaves when things aren't going too well for her."

She took another sip of her drink and placed the cup back on the table. "I suppose the one thing she does go on and on about is her on again, off again boyfriend, Steven somebody or other."

"He's a bad 'un, then?" asked Ant.

Jo focused on her teacup. "If you mean he is a fella who seems to come and go as he pleases, then, yes, in my mind he is a waste of space. I've told Kelly more than once to get rid of him, but we're not that close, so why should she take any notice of me?"

Lyn got up and walked the few paces to Jo and sat next to her on an impressively long settee. "It always is difficult to give advice when you're not sure the other person wants to hear the truth. Has she ever mentioned if Steven, how shall I put it, if Steven ever loses his temper with her?"

Go for the throat, why don't you.

Ant sensed Jo's unease and gave Lyn one of his looks.

She got the message. "It's okay, Jo, you're safe with us."

The planning officer took the opportunity to recover her cup and drink what remained of her tea. "I don't feel comfortable saying this, but there have been two or three occasions Kelly has come to work looking really upset. One time I brushed her arm, you know, to be supportive. Anyway, as soon as I touched her, she let out a yelp. Kelly didn't say anything and neither did I, but I'm sure you will draw the same conclusion that I did."

Ant remained quiet and left what was becoming an increasingly delicate conversation to the two women.

"Poor Kelly, what must she be going through?"

Jo shook her head. "I wouldn't waste too much sympathy on her. You said you knew one another, so you know just how vindictive that one can be. I, for one, would not like to get on the wrong side of her; she never seems to forget even the smallest slight at work, intended or not. I've seen Kelly purposely get a colleague into trouble with the boss just because she took a dislike to something they did. The horrible thing is it might be three or even six months later that she takes her revenge. It's horrible, so I make sure I keep out of the way as much as possible. I suppose if you want my honest opinion, she's ruthless. I imagine that means she will do very well in her career. She will use anyone and drop you in it if it suits her agenda; you know what it's like."

Ant sensed Jo becoming agitated. "You know, that was really brave of you and I can't tell you how helpful it may turn out to be. Now, I think we've kept you away from your funny marks long enough. How about we let you go?" He gave Jo a reassuring smile.

"Well, I just hope it's been of use to you both. You understand why I much prefer to spend my time looking for scratches on walls and in draughty attics?"

"I RATHER THINK Jo couldn't wait to get out of this room, and who could blame her?"

Lyn nodded. "The thing is, what do we do now?"

Ant finished off the last of his Danish and licked his fingers clean of any remnants of the pastry. "Let's just take a minute to go over what we know. For one, it's clear Steven Foster has a temper and is prepared to use physical force if need be. Kelly comes across as a calculating vengeance seeker, something you might agree with, thinking back to the bracelet issue. And then there's Lister. How does he fit into all of this?"

Lyn had only just stopped giving Ant the eye for licking his fingers. "What if the three of them are involved in some kind of conspiracy?"

Ant frowned. "You mean murder?"

"I'm not sure what I mean, but like it or not, those three

seem to be linked. Don't you think it a bit of a coincidence we were picked up by Lister just a few hours after my run-in with Kelly? Just saying."

The two friends fell silent as they tried to make sense of recent events.

"There is one thing we can do, Lyn. Steven Foster either alone or with Kelly and a nod from Lister were involved with Jack Spinner's death, never mind Amber's. It's got to be worth going back to the cottage. We might just get lucky."

Lyn began to tidy the teacups back onto the buffet. "Sounds a bit desperate, Ant."

He held his arms wide. "Any other ideas?"

"Look at that." Ant pointed to a clump of fallen branches amongst the trees.

Lyn muttered as she scrambled out of the Morgan, only to get tied up in some brambles as she stepped over the now familiar fallen log which disguised the track to Jack Spinner's bolthole. "Look at what?"

"A motorbike, there, can't you see it?"

Lyn smouldered with rage.

"All I see is the blood on both my shins from those stupid brambles."

Ant looked back to see his best friend dabbing her legs with a paper tissue. "It's only a scratch."

Lyn shot him her sternest head-teacher look. "I'll give you it's only a scratch. If ever anybody needed proof that I sweat blood for you, here it is. Now, just show me the bike instead of pointing into the trees."

He led the way, taking particular care to clear away any fine tree branches that might inflict further injury to his best friend. "Well, well, would you believe it? A Norton Dominator 500, quite a beast, and not for the faint hearted."

Lyn picked her way delicately through the undergrowth. "I have almost scratched myself to death to look at a silly motorbike?"

Ant gave a heavy sigh. "This isn't any old motorbike, it's a British classic and worth quite a bit of cash."

Lyn remained unimpressed. "Listen, it's up to you. We can either stand here while you get high on leaking engine oil or get to the cottage to see if we can find anything that can help us solve two murders. What's it going to be?"

Ant took one last lingering look at the black-and-chrome machine before retracing his steps as before, holding back any branches that might hit his partner. Within two minutes they stood on the edge of a clearing. In front of them the now familiar cottage stood looking as forlorn as ever.

"Can you hear anything?"

Lyn gave Ant one of her looks. "Not that again."

Ant frowned. "No, I mean it. I can hear something coming from behind the cottage?"

Lyn shrugged and began to move forward.

"Careful, Lyn. If there is anybody around, we don't want them to know we're here."

His advice was enough to slow Lyn. Walking in sync with one another, they advanced slowly, creeping around the far side of the cottage to get a view of what was going on without being seen.

They stood silent and scanned the area for any sign of movement.

"There," whispered Ant. "Look, somebody's moving in the outhouse where we discovered Jack Spinner. Now, who on earth would be disturbing a crime scene?"

Lyn gently bumped shoulders with her best mate. "Something tells me you are intent on finding out."

He smiled, then moved off towards the dilapidated timber building. "Are you coming or what?"

Lyn pointed an accusing finger at Ant as she silently closed the distance between them until they stood less than ten feet away from the broken-down entrance to the outhouse.

Readying himself for what was to come, he approached the entrance. In an instant, he leapt forward and grabbed the intruder. "Let me guess, your name is Steven Foster?"

Ant pulled the man by the collar until both stood outside the run-down construction.

"I'm saying nothing. Who are you, anyway? Let go before I make you sorry."

Ant laughed. "They said you had a temper; I wonder how far you would go to make your point. Murder, perhaps?"

The man continued his struggle as Ant kept a tight hold.

"What are you talking about, murder? Have you gone mad?"

Lyn interjected. "Then what are you doing here? Did Kelly send you?"

The man stopped struggling. "You know Kelly?"

Lyn came closer. "Do you not remember me, Steven? The way you mucked Amber about, the trouble you caused between her father and Jack Spinner who, incidentally, was found dead in the building. But perhaps you already knew that because you murdered him?"

The man studied his accuser. "Lyn Blackthorn. You always were a busybody, weren't you?"

Lyn smiled. "I suppose that's one way of putting it. I prefer to think I look out for people I care about."

Steven Foster smirked, leading Ant to give his collar a quick pull.

"Something amusing you?"

"Don't push me too far, mate. If I put my mind to it, I can take you, and her."

Ant gave the man another tug. "Can I just remind you who is holding whose collar."

Foster stopped struggling and shrugged his shoulders. "So, what now, Batman? Are you going to hand me over to the police? Oh, wait a minute, you shouldn't be here either."

Ant shot Lyn a serious look. She instinctively knew what he meant.

Realising Foster had put them in a corner and might well know more than he was letting on, Ant made his decision.

"I suggest you get out of this place and don't come back. And be careful who you threaten. I may not be the police, but there are very many dark forces the government use to get the results it wants. Do we understand one another?"

For the first time Foster looked genuinely alarmed. Ant loosened his grip and allowed the man to skulk away. Within a minute, the sound of a motorbike thundering in the near distance signalled that Foster had taken his leave.

Quiet returned to the cottage, which seemed at odds with its recent violent history.

"Should we carry on looking?"

And shook his head. "If you're right, and he's in cahoots with the others, he'll pull up at the first opportunity to contact Kelly, Lister, or both. We need to get out of here now."

As the Morgan sped away along the forested lane, Ant pressed the autodial on his mobile.

"Jemma, Ant here, listen, can you do me a favour? I need to know if you have anything on a man called Steven Foster."

Jemma Cole's voice sang out through the car's speaker system.

"It's the same Steven Foster that knocks around with Kelly Jarvis?"

"As I said earlier in the week, Jemma, there are no flies on you. Yep, that's our man. Can you check if he's known to the police and get back to me as soon as possible?"

"I can do better than that if you wait a few seconds. I'll plug his name into our online news and research archive."

"Wow, that's great." Ant looked across to Lyn. "Let's see what she comes up with."

Several seconds' silence came to an end as Jemma's voice floated through the air.

"I've got him. He's been quite a naughty boy. Two counts of burglary, one with violence. The odd thing is he seems to have been treated incredibly lightly by the courts. I guess it's about who you know, not what you know, right? Hope that's of some use to you? And don't forget, Anthony Stanton, you owe me another afternoon tea."

Ant disconnected the call and became aware that Lyn was quiet. He looked over to see her staring back at him. "What?"

"So, she's on speed dial, is she?"

Ant could feel himself blush. "I don't know what you mean, I mean—"

"Stop digging, Anthony, time to put the spade down."

The remainder of the drive back to Stanton Hall took

place largely in silence as Anthony thought through what to do next. He assumed Lyn was doing the same.

Then, out of nowhere, Lyn's voice pierced the warm summer air. "Look at that."

Taken aback by Lyn's sudden outburst, he instinctively turned to face her.

"Don't look at me, stupid, the other way."

As Ant turned to look at a layby on the opposite side of the road, he had a split second to glimpse two adults sitting in a car glaring straight back at him.

"What in heavens name is Kelly Jarvis doing in the same car as Commander Lister?"

16

CHAIN REACTION

I t wasn't often Ant visited his brother's grave. Today felt different. Perhaps the events of the last seven days had brought the untimely death of his older brother and associated pain, sadness, and a sense of loss to the fore. All he knew was that standing next to Greg's headstone and quietly talking to his elder sibling brought him at least a measure of peace.

Lost in thought, he didn't hear the sound of the ankle-high grass being disturbed.

"A penny for them?"

Ant looked around to see the familiar figure of Lyn smiling at him. "Ah, I've lost track of the days. I forgot it's Sunday morning. Off to church, are you?"

Lyn came closer and brushed his shoulder with her own. "Yes, you find comfort in coming to see your Greg; I get it from my weekly hour listening to Reverend Morton."

Ant didn't answer. Instead, he turned his attention back to the headstone. "What do you say, Greg. Is there anything to this religion malarkey?" He ran his hand across the top edge of the white marble, then patted it as though embracing his brother as they had done so often when they were growing up together.

Lyn stood silently by, reading the inscription for the hundredth time since Greg was interred.

"He had so much to live for, Lyn. Not least inheriting the Stanton Estate. One short journey that he took on a whim and look what happened."

She put a comforting arm around Ant. "I don't want to sound hard, but we have talked about that night so many times: what if you had done this, or that, he might still be alive. The brutal truth is it was Greg that decided to drive that evening. Not you, not your father or mother. Just Greg. You have to stop doing this, or you will hurt yourself, as if you haven't enough to be coping with from your time in the army."

Ant gently rubbed the back of Lyn's hand as it rested across his front. She was the only person in the world he would allow to get inside his head.

"I have a suggestion, and don't bite my head off. Why don't you come into church with me? You don't need to take part in the service, just immerse yourself in your own thoughts. If nothing else, it should be fun watching the vicar almost faint when he realises who the cat's dragged in."

Ant reflected on what his closest friend had said. He knew she would expect him to decline her offer as he always had in the past. But as he told himself again, today felt different. Gently releasing her embrace, Ant turned and began to feel unexpectedly awkward. "I suppose it saves me coming back for you later, and you never know, we might receive some divine inspiration to crack the case. Two conditions, though, I'm not singing or kneeling on those awful cushions."

Lyn tried in vain to suppress her delight. "It's a deal. Come on, before you change your mind." Her words were spoken softly as she gently pulled him by the hand through a maze of headstones leaning at crazy angles.

"Let's sit at the back, Lyn. That way I can nip out quietly if I've had enough."

Lyn touched his arm and resisted the urge to say anything he might take as criticism. "That's a good idea. I sometimes do that myself. You know what the Rev Morton can be like when he's in the mood."

"You did say this would only take an hour, didn't you?"

Lyn raised her eyebrows. "Like I said, it depends how the vicar's feeling, but yes, between forty-five minutes and an hour. Come on, let's sit here."

As he had expected, a number of heads swivelled to get a good look at who the people in the rear pew were. He was tempted to shout out and announce his presence to all concerned but thought better of the idea given the effect it might have on the vicar, not to mention Lyn.

Once the vicar had welcomed everybody to Sunday service, including a special mention for himself, which he could have done without, proceedings fell into their usual pattern. As ten minutes turned into twenty, Ant began to drift off and had to be gently poked more than once by Lyn to bring him back to his senses.

It was only when the Reverend Morton mentioned the subject of his sermon that his ears pricked up.

"This morning, my dear friends, I am going to talk to you about the sin of pride. In Proverbs 16:18, we are told that pride goes before destruction, a haughty spirit before a fall."

That's it, just as my father said. We have to confront him.

He turned to Lyn and whispered so energetically into

her ear that she recoiled slightly and lifted a finger to wipe away his enthusiasm.

"We've got to go, Lyn. I've got an idea, and there's no time to lose: come on."

Ant was already on his feet and making his way to the east door by the time Lyn had a chance to react.

"What on earth are you talking about, man. Confront who? Was the vicar really that bad? I thought his sermon was quite apt."

He smiled and clapped his hands.

"What have I told you about doing that hand-clapping thing? Not least we are stood immediately outside a place of worship with the service going on as we speak. Will you have some respect, please?"

"So you think you can bribe me with tea and cake to make up for dragging me out of church, do you?"

Ant had indeed decided that getting Lyn away from the clutches of the Reverend Morton's post-service get-together and out into the Norfolk countryside to talk her through his idea was indeed worth the price of a cappuccino and slice of millionaire's shortbread.

As they sat facing one another, each on a stainless-steel tubular chair separated by a small round table, Ant took in the quintessentially Norfolk Broads scene. A few yards behind them stood a small black-and-white-timbered café complete with thatched roof. Immediately to their front rested the sedate waters of Lowton Broad, its waters stretching left and right as far as the eye could see. On the other bank stood a busy boat-hire business with tourists moving between the equipment store and their chosen cruiser. To the left and in the mid-distance, an ancient stone road bridge arched over the water. Ant pondered how many tourists had fallen foul of its low headroom when passing under it for the first time.

"Anthony Stanton, I can see you're still in a world of your own and I have nearly finished my shortbread. So either buy me a second portion or I'm off to make my apologies to the vicar."

Lyn's rebuke brought him back to the realms of the real world. "You're forgetting, Lyn Blackthorn, you're in my car. It's got to be an hour's walk back to Stanton Parva."

Lyn began to bite. Mission accomplished, Ant leapt to his feet, smiled, and disappeared into the tiny wooden building. Within a minute he'd returned with two slices of the millionaire's shortbread, handed Lyn one, and sat down with the second. "I've also invested in two more teas, so I hope that paid my debt?"

Lyn started to give him one of her special looks before thinking better of it. "Okay, we have plenty of cake and enough tea to fill a bathtub. Now are you going to tell me what your bright idea is, or do I have to beat it out of you?"

Ant snapped his second piece of shortbread in half and took a great chunk of it into his mouth. "Do you remember the other day when my father said that Lister's ambition would be his undoing?"

Lyn's eyes lit up. "I see, now I understand. The vicar's sermon reminded you about your father's comments. Clever you, but what has that got to do with the price of fish?"

He almost choked on some shortbread crumbs as he tried to laugh and swallow at the same time.

"You do have some bad habits, Anthony Stanton. To think you went to public school."

Ant cleared his throat and took a sip of tea. "It's about all

I learnt at public school, and that's not saying much, is it. Anyway, back to Lister. We already know that three people seem to be linked through our investigation. What we don't know is what that link is. We have two questions to answer. First, what was Foster playing at rummaging around the cottage? Was he acting on his own behalf because he'd killed Jack Spinner? Or did somebody tell him what to look for? The second question is what is a senior officer in his mid-fifties doing in a car with a woman in her early thirties? Especially when the woman has an on again, off again boyfriend, Steven Foster?"

Lyn tucked into her shortbread without comment or raising her eyes from the tabletop.

"Did you hear a word of what I've just said?"

Lyn delicately dabbed away the crumbs from around her mouth and placed the paper napkin back onto the table. "Of course I did. But the thing is, we know most of this already, so how does your renewed enthusiasm, courtesy of a proverb about pride, move our investigations along? My take on things is that we will be lucky to stay on the outside of the jail cell, never mind solving the deaths of two wonderful people."

Ant made as if to clap his hands together again.

"Don't you dare."

"I was only joking; I knew you would say that. Well, on the face of things, you're correct. But we can sit here and wait for Lister to complete his little plan, or try to grab the initiative. Think about it, Lyn. Yes, he saw us yesterday, but he knows we clocked him. I've come across his type before. Lister will now go into overdrive to get us picked up again, so we need to take the fight to him."

Lyn gave her best friend a weary look. "Do you recall your father's barrister banging on and on the other day when he could have said what he wanted to say in about one-third of the time—your father hinted as much. Well, it seems you have caught the same affliction. Now, for the last time, tell me something I don't know and what you intend to do about it?"

"Like all the best plans, it's simple. I want you to get back in touch with Kelly Jarvis and do whatever you need to do to get yourself back in front of her. I don't know; tell her you found something out that she needs to know about, then when you get her on her own, don't spur the horses in pinning her ears to the wall to find out what her relationship with Lister is and how long it's been going on for."

Lyn tutted at her friend. "You are mixing your metaphors, Anthony Stanton."

"And you are getting on my nerves with your headteacher thing. If you don't stop, I shall clap again."

Lyn held up her arms in mock surrender. "And while I am running around like a mad fool, what does the great Lord Stanton intend to do?"

"Use exactly the same tactic on dear Commander Lister. Let's meet up over a drink back at Stanton Hall to compare notes. With a little luck either one of them will give something away that allows us to crack open this case."

As the pair left the table, Ant looked towards the bridge, raised his hand and waved at the two would-be twitchers. He gained great amusement from watching them hurriedly change the direction in which they were looking through the binoculars, with one of them overacting by enthusiastically pointing at some imaginary winged animal.

Well-practised in gaining access to the Morgan with its soft top down, Lyn scrambled over the low door and slipped into the passenger seat. Just as he was about to turn the ignition key, his mobile rang.

"For heaven's sake, it's Sunday lunchtime. Who on earth can this be?"

Lyn shrugged her shoulders. "I know it sounds obvious, but you won't know until you answer it, will—"

"Peter, how nice to hear from you; are you out with the dog?" He mouthed to Lyn that it was Detective Inspector Riley. "Yes, yes all is fine here. In fact we... Yes, I... What's that you say?"

Lyn's intrigue at what was occurring grew with each of Ant's half sentences.

"But that is incredible, almost unbelievable. Are you sure?"

It was too much for Lyn; she gave him a gentle prod with a finger. "What's he saying?"

Ant put a finger up to his closed lips, signalling for her to be quiet while he was listening. His gesture earned him a second prod of Lyn's finger.

"And have you written proof? Wow, that's incredible. Well done, Peter. Okay, I'll ring you back in about an hour once I've thought through exactly how to play this, and perhaps we can plan the endgame together? Yes, you too, Peter, and once again thank you for the call."

By now Lyn looked as if she would explode at any second in the absence of being told what Peter Riley had said.

Ant gave Lyn a sideways glance. "Let's just say neither of us need to run around after Lister or Kelly Jarvis. In fact, if my idea works out, quite the reverse. Now let's get you home, and I'll tell you exactly what we're going to do."

"What about the birdwatching goons?"

Ant pressed the Morgan's accelerator. "They don't stand a chance."

A BEAUTIFUL RED sky cradled the sinking sun as it kissed the North Sea horizon over Sidbourne Deep. All traces of a light summer breeze had melted away, leaving only the sound of the sea as it lazily lapped the foreshore, only to disappear beneath the glistening sands as it reached the high-water mark.

"Now, before you all think I've gone crazy, may I just thank you for coming out on a Sunday evening to stand in a cave on the north Norfolk coast. Of course, this place is familiar to all of you given the tragic events of last week." Ant looked to his right and gazed at the upturned boat that had failed to move an inch in the last seven days.

Gathered around him stood Kelly Jarvis, Steven Foster, Jemma Cole, and Commander Lister. Completing the assembly was Lyn, Fitch, and an elderly lady, who sat on a director's chair at the very back of the cave.

Commander Lister was the first to speak. "I assume the pair of you have a very good reason to have broken your bail conditions. You have exactly fifteen minutes to explain yourselves before I call my officers to have you arrested. Do I make myself clear?"

Ant looked at his wristwatch, tapped its face and turned his attention back to Lister. "If I may, this will take, I estimate, twenty minutes. Now, I think in the interests of justice and the effort everyone has made to be here this evening, I think we deserve an extra five minutes." He turned his attention from Lister to Kelly Jarvis without giving the commander time to respond. "I should like to offer my special thanks to Miss Kelly Jarvis and her beau, Steven Foster, since it has been a very stressful week for both of them. Of course, the same goes... Well, I think I'm correct in saying the same goes for all of us."

Ant saw that, not unexpectedly, both Kelly and Steven looked particularly uncomfortable, and it was noticeable that Miss Jarvis kept her distance from Commander Lister: neither made any attempt to acknowledge the other.

"Last Saturday, a young woman was found inside that boat out there. At first, we assumed she had died in a sailing accident. After all, the evening before, one of the most vicious storms to hit the north coast raged for hours. You might ask what anybody was doing in a tiny boat in such outrageous weather. Well, once the immediate shock of turning that vessel over and finding the body of an innocent woman subsided, Lyn and I began to think the same."

Lister folded his arms tight across his chest. "All this is remarkably interesting, I'm sure. Nevertheless, this isn't getting us anywhere, and you have fifteen minutes before I make that phone call."

Ant smiled. "It's interesting that you put so much importance on time, Commander Lister. My father always says that time waits for no man. I prefer to look at that another way and think that time catches up with us all. I think that is particularly relevant to you, Commander Lister."

Lister fumed. "That's enough, how dare you speak to a senior police officer in that way. I promised your father I would involve you in this case, and I have been as good as my word, and this is how you repay me?"

The sound of several people coughing reverberated around the jagged stone walls of the cave as the nervous tension increased.

"If you might forgive me, Commander Lister, you have done precisely the opposite, even going so far as to arrest Lyn and me. What type of cooperation is that? Anyway, I digress. Not only do we have the death of Amber Burton to deal with, but the second tragedy occurred a few days ago. As we know, her long-term boyfriend, Jack Spinner, was found dead at an isolated cottage which, it seems, he and Amber had occupied for several years. So let's take things in the order that they happened. Ten years ago, Amber Burton and her boyfriend took to his jet ski. It was understood there had been a tragic accident and Amber was lost. A few days later, Jack Spinner also disappeared. Now, despite the best endeavours of the then Detective Inspector Lister, no trace of either was found and the case file was closed."

"But what has that got to do with my boyfriend and me?"

Ant held his finger as if he'd hatched a sudden idea. "A good point, Kelly. After all, we are told you were Amber's best friend. And yet... and yet it seems you are the jealous sort, more than that, someone who never forgot being put down whether real or imagined. You have a reputation, Kelly, for getting your own back. What's the saying? 'Vengeance is best served cold'? From what I can gather, you are an expert in such things."

Ant noticed Foster begin to move. "Stay there, young man. If I wish you to move, I'll tell you. Do we understand each other?" Ant smiled as he watched Foster skulk backwards.

"As you have just demonstrated, Mr Foster, you, too, have a temper. May I suggest it sometimes gets the better of you and you hit whoever is nearest. Isn't that right, Kelly?"

Kelly Jarvis instinctively moved a few inches away from her boyfriend. "I have no idea what you're talking about."

"So here we have three people connected to each other not just by recent events, as we shall discover in a few minutes, but also a conspiracy that directly led to Amber Burton and Jack Spinner colluding to disappear off the face of the earth. Now imagine what that meant, particularly for Amber. She had lost her mother some years previously and was having a difficult relationship with her father. Yet she knew him to have been a hard-working, decent, and loving father before he lost his wife. A difficult situation for any teenager to have to deal with. Yet she did have to deal with more... a great deal more. Is it true, Steven, that you were Amber's boyfriend before Jack Spinner appeared on the scene? Let me answer that for you. Indeed you were, and we mentioned a little while ago about how jealous you can get at times. And you, Kelly. You, too, have a vicious streak. Something happened between Amber and you, and unless you tell us, perhaps we'll never find out. But whatever it was, that led to you making a play for Mr Foster here, who in turn was intent on making Amber pay for, as he saw it, belittling him."

Lister began to take his mobile from his jacket pocket. "A few minutes longer if you will, Commander." Ant's rebuke caused the senior officer to replace his mobile. "Time is running out for both you and Miss Blackthorn; you just remember that."

"Oh, I don't know, Commander. Remember what I said about time catching up with us all? I reckon you have another two or three minutes. And then there's the strange case of the stolen bracelet. It seems Kelly did her good deed for the day just before Amber and Jack disappeared by handing Lyn's jacket back to her that she left in the chip shop. The only problem was the police conveniently turned up and, even more peculiarly, the bracelet was found in one of Lyn's jacket pockets."

Kelly protested. "It wasn't me that called the police, and I didn't put anything in anybody's pocket."

"Perhaps you did or you didn't, but somebody planted

that bracelet. The thing that struck me was who did the bracelet belong to in the first place?"

"It was mine; I bought the bracelet."

Ant tilted his head towards Kelly. "But you couldn't provide a receipt for the police, could you?"

Kelly fell silent. Ant observed a cold stir being exchanged between Steven Foster and Kelly.

"So, Commander Lister, it brings me back to you. Thanks to the intrepid work of our local reporter, I discovered that somehow you managed to convince the magistrate to be overly lenient when it came to sentencing our Steven here."

Lister exploded. "What are you accusing me of? Be very, very careful what you say next."

"It is true that you were involved in prosecuting Steven Foster twice ten years ago, is it not? Now, one of those criminal actions involved violence, so how come he got off so lightly?"

Lister shot Steven Foster a cold, sharp look. Ant recognised immediately it was a warning for Foster to keep his mouth shut.

"You see I think it suited your purposes to have somebody with a temper. Somebody not afraid to use violence who was in hock to you. Who could say when such an asset might come in handy? As for Kelly, she was a useful fool for you, wasn't she? You could have pressed charges against her for the disappearing bracelet, but you didn't. After all, she admitted she'd bought it yet couldn't provide any proof of purchase or where she'd bought it from. Yet you decided to let the matter slip. Worse than that, you were prepared to see an innocent young girl, Lyn Blackthorn, prosecuted for theft. It was only the diligent work by one of your officers, in fact the only officer, still here from your spell in Stanton

Parva, that saw the matter dropped, and that's how you brought Kelly Jarvis under your very dark wing."

For the first time that evening, Fitch spoke. "Forgive me if I'm being thick, but are you saying the good commander was blackmailing these two?"

Ant shrugged his shoulders. "Blackmail, coercion, demanding favours with menaces, take your pick what you call it, but nevertheless it worked in getting Amber and her boyfriend to disappear in a panic. It also worked in frightening Lyn Blackthorn half to death, and all things being equal, that would have been the end of it."

Jemma Cole stepped forward. "So you're telling us that these three murdered both Amber and Jack Spinner?"

Ant shook his head. "Not directly, though because of the inaction of Commander Lister, Jack Spinner was killed. Isn't that right Steven?"

Foster froze. "I didn't murder anybody. Yes, I admit I did a few things for him because he got me off those two charges, but murder? They weren't down to me."

Lyn pushed herself gently off the wall she'd been leaning against. "So that just leaves you, Kelly, or should I say Commander Lister and you."

Lister recovered his mobile from a pocket and began to tap a keypad. At the other end of the cave Kelly became hysterical.

"I didn't murder anybody. It was him. He controlled us ten years ago. It started again when he came back last week. These murders are nothing to do with me. I can't speak for Steven Foster, but all I did was to wind Lyn up because he told me to and to keep an eye on what you were up to."

Just then Ant's mobile pinged to signify a text message. He looked at the screen, then Lyn, and nodded and moved towards the entrance.

"I wouldn't make that call just yet, Commander. In fact, I will oblige you by calling for police officers myself in just under two minutes."

Lister sneered at Ant. "We shall see, Lord Stanton. We shall see."

"Indeed we shall, Commander Lister. Ah, perfect timing."

Several heads turned towards the cave entrance; someone could be heard crunching on the gravel just outside.

"Do come and join us, Thomas."

Commander Lister froze.

A solitary figure appeared in silhouette, backlit by the fading sun. Ant signalled to Fitch and Lyn. A split second later the cave was bathed in a soft light as a number of torches illuminated Beggars Cave.

"What the devil are you doing here?" Lister's voice had risen at least one octave.

The figure came closer. "You told me to meet you here, Dad."

Fitch and Jemma let out a gasp. "He has a son?" said Fitch incredulously.

From the back of the cave, the old lady made her presence known. Standing from her director's chair, she pointed a finger at the cave entrance. "That is the man. He is the one I saw in my garden with a young woman last Friday evening."

"Can you be certain?" said Ant.

"Oh yes, he's the one." The old lady fell silent and resumed her seat.

Commander Lister strode over to his son and placed a hand on each of the man's shoulders. "Why did you come?"

Thomas Lister looked at his father. "But you told me to come."

Lister shook his head. "This won't do. You have us here under false pretences, and I intend to see you prosecuted, Stanton."

A second person penetrated the cave entrance. "I think not, Commander Lister. At least that's the rank you hold for the time being, though I would suggest both that and your police pension are about to go up in smoke."

Detective Inspector Riley strode confidently into the softly lit space, followed by his desk sergeant. "You thought you were being clever by chucking me out of my office to undermine my authority and calling in all of the archived records pertaining to Amber Burton's apparent death. Paranoia is an awful thing, so when you also locked the computer files, my sergeant and I began to do a little digging."

"You're a fool, Riley. Who in heaven's name listens to you?"

"Sadly for you, a combination of my officer unearthing, quite by accident, the one piece of information that could implicate you, together with the trust of Lord Stanton and Lyn Blackthorn, we were able to track down your son and encourage him to meet you here this evening."

Lister spat his venom at Riley. "This is all nonsense. Steven Foster murdered Amber Burton, then covered his tracks by murdering Jack Spinner and I will prove it."

Detective Inspector Riley laughed. "Your days of planting evidence, fitting people up, and bullying those that won't comply with your wishes are over. That piece of information I spoke about was a witness statement from Amber Burton a few weeks before she disappeared. Amber raised a complaint against the young man who was harassing her. I use the term harassing' as a polite description for what your son, Thomas Lister, attempted to do to Amber. When she refused his advances, he started to threaten both her and her boyfriend. Of course, as the investigating officer, it was the one time your separation from your wife played to your advantage because she took Thomas with her. Unfortunately, he decided to revisit the village since he was obsessed with Amber Burton."

Ant stepped forward so he was standing just inches away from the commander's face. "And you used your tricks and influence to inveigle Kelly Jarvis and Steven to do your bidding. That gave you time to get your son out of the way, confuse matters with the odd behaviour between Kelly, Amber, and an unknowing Lyn Blackthorn, and the job was done. He forced Amber and Jack to plan their escape, and as far as anybody was concerned, it had been a case of an unfortunate accident and an inconsolable boyfriend."

Lister took a step back. "This is simply nonsense. You have no evidence other than a scrap of paper not contained within the file it apparently pertains to, and which is uncorroborated. Let's call an end to this nonsense now."

Ant clapped his hands together. For once, Lyn appeared to have no objection. The remainder of his audience ducked in unison as if the cave were about to collapse.

"Well, I suppose we could always call for Morris?"

"Have you gone mad, man. What on earth are you talking about?"

"A fair question, Commander Lister. I refer, of course, to my dear friend's cat who seems to have taken somewhat of a disliking to your son."

Thomas Lister's reaction caused consternation; a general hubbub erupted which Lister and his son tried to take advantage of by advancing to the cave entrance. Only the burly frame of the desk sergeant prevented their escape.

"Thomas, may I see your right shin, please?" Ant's strange request caused an eerie silence to fall. Lister's son looked worried and confused.

"Don't be shy, Thomas. If, as you say, you have nothing to do with Amber Burton's death, it will be because you were never on the cliffs above this cave, and the cat didn't attack you. If, on the other hand, there are signs of injury consistent with an animal's claws, well, that will be another thing altogether."

Thomas Lister looked at his father.

"It's no use looking at Dad; you're a big boy now. Please, your right shin?"

Thomas moved towards Ant as slowly as his legs could carry him. Haltingly, he bent forward and rolled up his trouser leg. There, for all to see, were several parallel scratch marks running vertically down the side of his leg from just below his kneecap to slightly above his ankle."

Lyn suddenly shouted. "Chain, his chain. Look at his chain, Ant."

Ant smiled. "Well spotted, Lyn. I, too, noticed the jewellery around his neck."

Thomas Lister instinctively tried to button his open-collared shirt.

"Too late now, Thomas. Please allow me." Ant leant forward, reached out a hand, and gently pulled the remainder of the man's chain from his chest. On the end dangled a small charm.

Lyn ran forward and grabbed the chain, causing Thomas to tip forward. "It's Amber's. That's part of the charm I gave her and was the piece I found in the gravel by her body last week."

Thomas Lister looked at his father this time almost in tears.

"Don't say anything, son. Nothing at all."

Riley's desk sergeant closed in on Lister's son.

Ant pointed at Thomas. "Somehow you found out where Amber and Jack were living. Unless you tell us, perhaps we'll never know how you came by that information. But unfortunately for you, somebody spotted you. But I mustn't tease. In fact, it was me, although I didn't know that at the time."

"So that's why you nearly crashed your silly camper van," said Lyn.

Ant laughed. "Sort of, I was convinced it was Commander Lister out of uniform, but then it didn't make sense and I dismissed it as a mistake. It was only in the last couple of days I began to think about it again. When Peter Riley rang me earlier today, it all made sense. It wasn't Commander Lister I saw; it was his son. As we can see, they share many of the same facial characteristics.

"So what happened last Friday night, and then with Jack Spinner?" asked Fitch.

"Once Thomas had tracked Amber down, somehow, he managed to get her away from Jack. It's difficult to imagine he used charm to persuade her to go with him to the clifftops, since he seems completely devoid of that attribute. So I have to conclude that he forced her. Perhaps he threatened to hurt Jack if she didn't do what he wanted. In any event, the two of them ended up on that clifftop. My theory is that he tried to press himself as he had done ten years previously. Poor Amber resisted as she had done back then too, before he lost his temper. He lashed out and she toppled over the cliff.

"But how did she get into the boat?" asked Fitch.

"That was an absolute gift for him, I suspect. Once he got over the shock and looked over the cliff, he saw the small vessel and knew at once he could make Amber's death look like a boating accident. After all, a storm was raging, and who would miss someone who supposedly died ten years earlier?"

"And that's why Jack Spinner had to die?" said Jemma.

Ant turned to the reporter. "Exactly. Jack was the only one who knew Amber wasn't dead before last Saturday. Thomas Lister couldn't take the chance of him speaking out, so he murdered him, and I suspect his father tried to frame Steven Foster so he could make his son do his disappearing act for a second time."

Thomas Lister started to shout. "I told you, Dad. I told you not to make me kill Spinner. Amber was an accident. We could have got away with that, but no, as usual, everyone has to do exactly as you order them. It's your fault, Dad. Not mine."

"WELL, Peter, what a hero you turned out to be. If it hadn't been for you, Lyn and I would have taken off at the speed of light to try and fool Kelly Jarvis and Commander Lister into spilling the beans. I know now that they'd have tied us up in knots, we'd probably have ended up in jail, and Steven Foster would have been the fall guy for two murders. What can I say?"

Detective Inspector Riley blushed as Ant patted him on the back, and the assembled crowd in the Wherry Arms gave a round of applause. In the corner sat Amber's father adding a solemn, but dignified presence to the proceedings.

"Thank you for those kind words, Anthony, but it was my

desk sergeant who did the spade work. If it hadn't been for Fred's tenacity, things might have turned out quite differently."

All eyes turned to Fred, who lifted up his pint in acknowledgement.

Ant grabbed hold of Peter Riley's hand and shook it with a firm grip. "I know we often haven't seen eye to eye, and I think I'm rather to blame for that, so here's to a new start. Ant pulled a surprised Riley into him for a man hug.

The bar broke into a riot of laughter.

"Come on, you two, you'll be getting engaged next," said Fitch. A chorus of cheers followed as the two men smiled awkwardly at each other.

Fitch turned to Lyn. "Are you prepared to be two-timed, then?"

Lyn beamed a particular smile at Ant. Anthony Stanton gave the same intimate smile back. He walked over to where she was standing."So how are you doing, Ms Blackthorn?"

Lyn linked his arm and gave him a quizzical look. "One question I've been burning to ask you."

"What's that?" replied Ant.

"Why exactly did you drag me to Sandringham House last Saturday?"

Ant's smile faded. "My old commanding officer asked to see me. As you could tell, he moves in rarefied circles. He wanted to sound me out for resuming active service, and I guess he was trying to impress me with the surroundings."

The bar fell into a stony silence as his words reverberated around the small space. Lyn's smile disappeared to be replaced by a tear-filled glare at Ant.

"And?" she whispered.

Ant's face broke into a broad smile. "I told him I had more important matters to attend to here. I'm not going anywhere, Lyn, at least not without you. Now give me a hug."

The bar once more echoed to the sound of affectionate cheering.

END

ENGLISH (UK) TO US GLOSSARY

- **Bitter Shandy:** A pint of beer comprising 50% beer and 50% lemon-soda
- **Broad:** A stretch of shallow water formed from old peat diggings. Common in Norfolk and Suffolk regions of the UK. Can take the form of narrow stretches of water-like canals, or open water like small lakes.
- **Butty:** Slang term for sandwich
- **Clocked (him):** Slang for being discovered, found out, observed. "I clocked you getting into your car."
- **Cop it:** Slang term for getting in trouble, e.g. 'If you don't stop throwing stones you're going to cop it [from the police, parent or other authority]
- **Dossed:** Sleep in rough accommodation or on street. "He dossed down."
- **Drop you in it:** UK slang for getting someone into trouble by telling tales or 'accidentally' passing information to a superior/parent etc.

- **Flitting:** Moving quickly from place to place
- **Fiver:** Everyday slang term for five British pounds banknote
- **A Full English:** Slang term to denote a traditional cooked breakfast comprising (usually) bacon, sausage, beans, hash browns, tomatoes, mushrooms, toast and butter and/or fried bread, eggs. Regional variations apply
- **Gazumped:** Outbid for a house by a later, higher offer, once yours has already been accepted by the vender
- **Hoi Polloi:** Pronounced 'hoy-pal-oy', Old English term used by aristocrats for 'lower-class' people in UK. Meant as term of derision
- **House of Lords:** Upper Chamber of UK Parliament equivalent to US Senate
- **Kitchen Roll:** Paper Towels
- **Listed Building:** A legal categorisation (Government maintained list) of buildings and other pieces of architecture in England and Wales that are considered important and cannot be altered without official permission. There are three grades with Grade II being the lowest, Grade II* being the next most important and Grade I representing the rarest/most important buildings.
- **On the QT:** Slang term for clandestine activities, "Better do this on the QT or James will get to hear about it."
- **Packs-in:** When an item breaks down or ceases to work, e.g. "The fridge has packed-in, we'll need a new one."
- **Public Schools** are, in fact, 'private' schools

where parents pay the full cost of education for their child instead of them attending 'state-school'

- **Pulling the Wool:** Traditional term used for someone trying to trick others: To hoodwink
- **Quag:** Marshy ground, 'a quagmire' derived for Viking Scandinavian word Kwag
- **Rib:** Idiom for teasing or joking someone
- **Scallywag:** Old-fashioned, light-hearted term for someone who continually misbehaves. "He's a scallywag, that one."
- **Skiff:** Traditional name for small boats used for coastal sailing
- **Special Branch:** Arm of UK police service, which works closely with the intelligence service like the US FBI
- **Sweets:** Candy
- **Tasburgh:** Norfolk village pronounced 'Tase-ber-er'
- **The City:** Traditional name for London's financial district
- **The Price of Fish:** Slang term used when someone says something that has nothing to do with the topic of a conversation.
- **Tomato Sauce:** Ketchup/Catsup
- **Wherry:** A traditional sailboat used for carrying goods and passengers on the Norfolk & Suffolk Broads
- **Wymondham:** Name of Norfolk Market-town pronounced 'Wind-em'

AFTERWORD

Did You Enjoy Dead Again?

Reviews are so important in helping get my books noticed. Unlike the big, established authors and publishers, I don't have the resources available for big marketing campaigns and expensive book launches (though I live in hope!).

What I _do_ have, gratefully, is the following of a loyal and growing band of readers.

Genuine reviews of my writing help bring my books to the attention of new readers.

If you enjoyed this book, it would be a great help if you could spare a couple of minutes and kindly head over to my Amazon page to leave a review (as short or long as you like). All you need do is click on one of the links below.

UK

US

All other Territories

Thank you so much.

Join My Readers' Club

Getting to know my readers is the thing I like most about writing. From time to time I publish a newsletter with details on my new releases, special offers, and other bits of news relating to the Norfolk Murder Mystery series. If you join my Readers' Club, I'll send you this gripping short story free and ONLY available to club members:

A Record of Deceit

Grace Pinfold is terrified a stranger wants to kill her. Disturbing phone calls and mysterious letters confirm the threat is real. Then Grace disappears. Ant and Lyn fear they have less than forty-eight hours to find Grace before tragedy strikes, a situation made worse by a disinterested Detective Inspector Riley who's convinced an innocent explanation exists.

Character Backgrounds

Read fascinating interviews with the four lead characters in the Norfolk Cozy Mysteries series. Anthony Stanton, Lyn Blackthorn, Detective Inspector Riley, and Fitch explain what drives them, their backgrounds, and let slip an insight into each of their characters. We also learn how Ant, Lyn, and Fitch first met as children and grew up to be firm friends even if they do drive each other crazy most of the time!

You can get your free content by visiting my website at www.keithjfinney.com

I look forward to seeing you there.

Keith

Dedication

For Joan, who is always there for me.

ACKNOWLEDGMENTS

Acknowledgements

Cover design by Keith Finney

Line Editor: Paula
    paulaproofreader.wixsite.com/home

Proof Reader:
    Terrance Grundy of Editerry

My Wonderful Advance Reader Group

Jo, who pre-empted the setting of this book and agreed to feature (in a fictional sense) to being a character - she's one of the goodies!

ALSO BY KEITH FINNEY

In the Norfolk Murder Mystery Series:

Dead Man's Trench

Narky Collins, Stanton Parva's most hated resident, lies dead at the bottom of an excavation trench. Was it an accident, or murder?

Amateur sleuths, Ant and Lyn, team up to untangle a jumble of leads as they try to discover the truth when jealousy, greed, and blackmail combine in an explosive mix of lies and betrayal.

Will the investigative duo succeed, or fall foul of Detective Inspector Riley?

Murder by Hanging

Ethan Baldwin hangs from a tree in woods just outside the quiet Norfolk village of Stanton Parva. The police think the respected church warden committed suicide. **Ant and Lyn are certain someone murdered Ethan and set out to bring his ruthless killer to justice.**

Suspects include a greedy land developer, a vicar in turmoil, and a businessman about to lose everything.

Can our amateur sleuths solve the crime, or will the killer get away scot-free?

The Boathouse Killer

Successful businessman, Geoff Singleton, is found dead in the cabin of his cruiser on the Norfolk Broads. His wife's ex-partner suddenly appears, and a secret which someone does not want exposed merge into a countdown to catastrophe.

When the body of a respected young entrepreneur is discovered, sat bolt upright with unseeing eyes, Detective Inspector Riley concludes it's a heart attack.

Ant and Lyn are suspicious; why would a fit man suddenly die? *The deeper they dig, the more the inconsistencies mount.* Convinced the police are wrong, the pair have just days to identify the killer before DI Riley turns on them with the threat of arrest for perverting the course of justice. *Will the killer be exposed? Or will their evil scheming pay off?*

Miller's End

Forty-five minutes ago, the owner of an ancient Norfolk windmill joked happily with his visitors. *Now he's dead. An innocent accident or murder? Time is running out to uncover the truth.*

Burt Bampton lived for his work - and preserving Norfolk's heritage. How could a man used to skipping up and down the mill's narrow stairs suddenly slip and fall?

Detective Inspector Riley believes it to be a tragic accident.

Ant and Lyn think different, and as disturbing coincidences begin to emerge all the evidence points to murder. **Greed, jealousy and betrayal** take our amateur sleuths on a baffling journey to uncover the appalling truth.

Set in the evocative landscape of Norfolk, this compelling cozy murder mystery, with its thread of humour and hint of romance between our two lead characters will keep you on the edge of your seat until the very end.

If you like the Faith Martin, Joy Ellis or Betty Rowland's Mysteries, then you'll love Keith Finney's Norfolk Cozy Mystery thrillers.

www.keithjfinney.com

Facebook

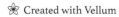

Printed in Great Britain
by Amazon

55857827R00132